HAIR SECRETS

Karina Chapman

Also by

K M Chapman

The Vixens' Secret Handbook:

Arleia—Adventure Vixen

HAIR SECRETS

Karina Chapman

Hair Secrets

ISBN: 978-0-6481111-2-2 (hc)
ISBN: 978-0-6481111-0-8 (pbk)
ISBN: 978-0-6481111-1-5 (ebk)

This hardcover edition published by Kaycee Energy Publishing.

Books can be ordered by contacting the publisher:
Website: www.kmchapmanauthor.com
Email: contact@kmchapmaauthor.com

Editing: www.thewriterssurgeon.com
Layout Design: www.doctorzed.com

Kaycee Energy Publishing rev. date 05/11/2017

Acknowledgements

I would like to thank the following people for their invaluable help, belief and support along the journey of writing this book.

To my fantastic and supportive family, friends and clients who believed I could put pen to paper, and had to listen to me talk about hair and writing much more than I'm sure they ever wanted to!

To the late Diane Beer; you are still a totally fabulous, inspirational soul. Thank you for your wonderful input and help, the journey would have been nowhere near as fruitful or fun without you.

To God and the universe, who gave me the inspiration and ability to create this book to help others.

May you all enjoy fabulous hair days every day!

Karina

"A woman who cuts her hair is about to change her life."

Coco Chanel

Contents

Introduction

Sick of fighting the frizz, being bamboozled by product choices or need to know what's going to work for your hair? Do you get those *'Bad Hair'* days when your hair displays a mind of its own and nothing you do will make it behave?

There is nothing worse than when your hair looks and feels fantastic as you walk out of the hair salon, but you can never get it to look the same yourself at home.

This book has been written to help women of any age, with all levels of hair styling skills to look and feel good about their hair every day.

You will learn to:

- Banish bad hair days forever
- Know what colors and hair styles will suit you best
- Use your straighteners to curl or straighten
- Fight dry, frizzy hair successfully
- Avoid hair disasters
- Find a new stylist easily
- Choose the right type of products for your hair
- Know why hair loss occurs and why
- Blow dry and style 'big hair'

It's about sharing with you the right knowledge, right products and right tools so that you can fix those annoying 'bad hair' days every time, and look great between hairdressing visits.

After working in the hairdressing industry for over twenty-five years I have lots of helpful knowledge to share. Apart from owning two salons,

I was also a college lecturer teaching both apprentice hairdressers and retraining qualified hairdressers.

During this time I've gathered information on all aspects of hair-care and styling. And most importantly what works and what doesn't, as well as gaining extensive knowledge about the common problems that frustrate most women about their hair.

While giving advice to a client about hair loss one day, I found I was constantly answering many of the same questions from different clients.

Questions like: "*How do I stop my hair from frizzing*?" Or "*Do I really need to use a heat protecting product before straightening*?" And "*What hair style would suit my face?*"

We all know what it's like to hate your hair at times. Even if you are wearing your favorite outfit and makeup is done to perfection – if your hair isn't right - you don't feel happy!

I realized there was a need for helpful information to be shared with women, to help you look and feel your best every day.

This book will answer your questions and share hairdressing secrets to take the worry out of '*Bad Hair*' days.

All the tips in this book are easy to follow. With the right information on correct tools, instructions and products for your type of hair, you will be able to fix hair problems and enjoy fabulous looking hair every day! Sounds like a dream, doesn't it?

I promise this will be easy, no matter what level of skill you have with managing your hair now. Let's get started!

Karina

1. What's Your Hair Type?

When I ask a client what type of hair they have, they generally describe their hair as thick or thin. Technically I want to determine the diameter of each strand of hair.

Why is this important to know? Because knowing whether the texture of your hair is fine or coarse will help you choose the right products for your hair.

FINE HAIR – has a small diameter, and can break easily when put under stress. It can be flyaway, slow growing and look limp or greasy at times. When in good condition, the fine hairs cuticle layer (the outside layer of the hair) is smooth, which makes fine hair appear shiny naturally.

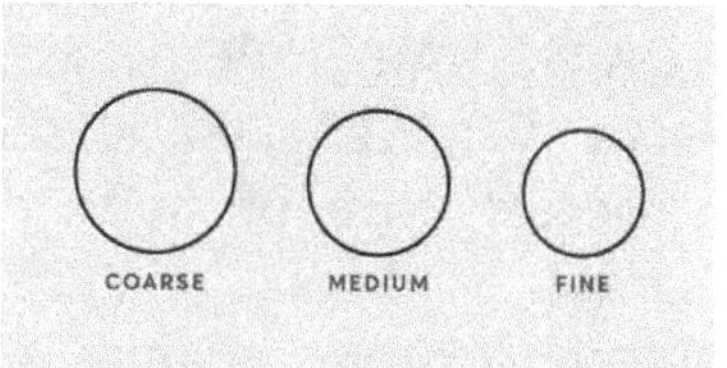

Things that dry out, weaken or break fine hair are:

- High lift blondes, bleaches or perms
- Straightening irons on too high a temperature setting
- Bleach that is messily applied, overlapping onto previously bleached hair which causes a weak spot in the hair where the strand is susceptible to break
- Using hot tools without a heat protective product, or leaving heat on fine hair in one spot for too long
- Hairdryers set on too hot a setting

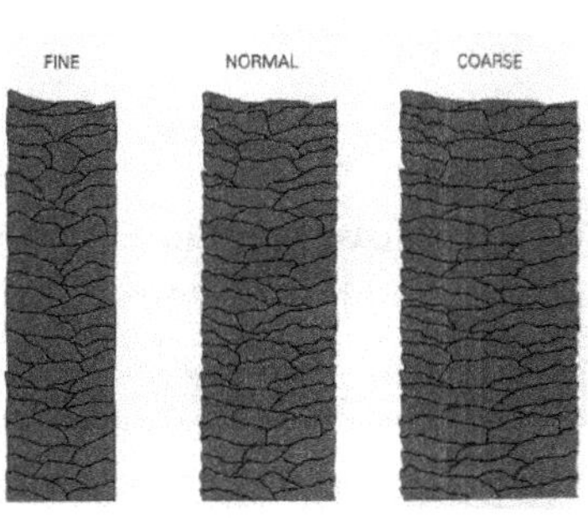

MEDIUM HAIR TYPE – has a medium diameter, is stronger and can handle more stress than fine hair, although it can still break. Medium hair types are naturally shiny when straight, but can appear duller if the natural curl frizzes. Medium textured hair which is wavy or curly tends to go fluffy if the hair is dry in condition.

Things that will dry out, weaken or break medium hair are:

- Bleach or perms left on your hair too long
- Bleach or light blonde colors applied over hair that has already been bleached or lightened
- Straightening irons left on one section of hair too long, or without a heat protective product
- Hairdryers set on too hot in one section of hair for too long

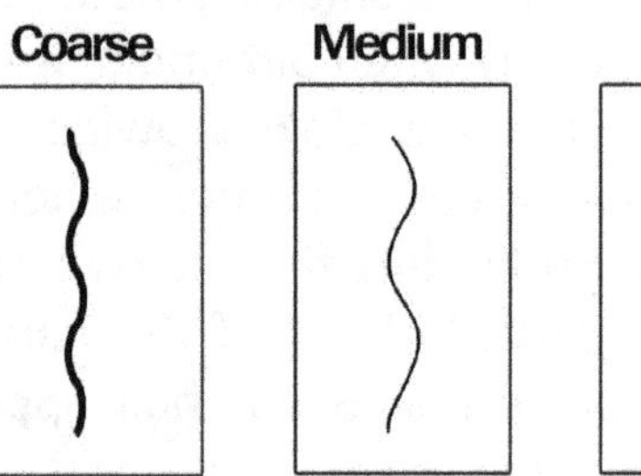

COARSE HAIR TYPE – has a large diameter, and is the strongest type of hair. It's harder to break and can handle more punishing chemical services (bleaching and perming) than the smaller fine and medium hair types. The outside layer (or cuticle layer) tends to be raised, which can make coarse hair appear less shiny.

Things that will dry out, weaken or break coarse hair are:

- Continuous bleaching and overlapping of bleach applications
- Straightening irons left on one section too long
- Hairdryers on the hottest heat setting left on any one section of the hair too long

The other helpful thing to know is whether you have a sparse, medium or dense amount of hair growing on your head. You will usually already know that by the feel of your hair, or from conversations with your hairdresser.

You may have coarse hair; but only a sparse amount per square centimeter growing on your scalp. Or you could have fine hair, but a huge number of hairs per square centimeter or inch growing on your scalp. This makes your hair appear thick because of the quantity of hairs on your head, even though your hair is fine in texture.

This sketch shows a bob style with fine hair that's sparse in amount per square inch. This hair type looks the thinnest and often needs more volume added when blow drying, and stronger products to maintain the style through the day.

This face shape is the same as the first. It shows the same bob style still with fine hair, but where there are a lot of hairs per square inch growing.

The hair is fine in texture, but when there's more hair per square inch growing, the head of hair has a lot more natural body than in the first example with less hairs per square inch.

This third sketched comparison of hair types shows a layered flick out style with **fine hair** that has a medium amount of hairs growing per square inch on her scalp.

Our fourth example shows a layered flick out style. With **coarse hair** where there is a medium of hair per square inch; so it appears thick in amount and has more volume naturally.

This sketch shows a long curly style with **fine hair** that has a medium in amount of hairs growing per square centimeter. Because of its curl it appears naturally fuller.

This sketch depicts a long curly style with **coarse hair** where a sparse quantity of hair per square inch grows. So there are less hairs but still a lot of volume and body.

The final sketch here demonstrates how a long curly style with **coarse hair** with a lot of hairs growing looks. So it's high in the number of hairs growing as well as being coarse in texture. This type of hair is often thinned out by stylists to avoid looking like a wig.

Now that you have worked out your hair type and thickness lets move on to figuring out your face shape!

2. A Guide to Face Shapes

Have you ever wondered why face shapes are important when choosing the right style to suit you? Do you know what shape your face is? An experienced hairdresser always considers your face shape before designing a style to suit you.

SECRET STYLING TIP #1

Make sure that your finished style makes your face appear oval shaped. This applies whenever you are styling your hair or choosing a new hairstyle.

Why oval? It's because it has been scientifically proven that human beings find oval face shapes the most attractive. I've tested this theory hundreds of times on different female face shapes over the years, and every time the client loves the finished result much more when I make her face appear oval.

You know what it's like to have one of those annoying hair days. You style your hair exactly the same every day, yet some days you don't like the result as much as you liked it yesterday! You have the feeling something's wrong with it but you can't tell what.

When this happens, check in the mirror to assess how your face looks with that style. Is your style today making your face appear oval shaped? Or is it looking like a square? Possibly triangular, oblong or round shaped?

To make your hair look better so that you feel happier with your finished result, slightly adjust your finished style to create an oval face shape. I have included some examples for you later in the book.

The most common different types of face shapes are:

- Oval
- Round
- Square
- Oblong
- Triangular
- Heart

To find out which shape closest fits your face, pull all your hair off your face and secure with a headband. That will make it easier to see the exact shape of your face.

Now assess the shape that nearest fits yours.

Once you know your face shape it will be easier to know the styles that will suit you best. Here are a few tips on what works or what to avoid with each face shape.

OVAL

Lucky you! This is the best face to be able to wear no fringe, and be able to pull your hair back in a ponytail and still look great. Almost any style looks great when you have an oval face.

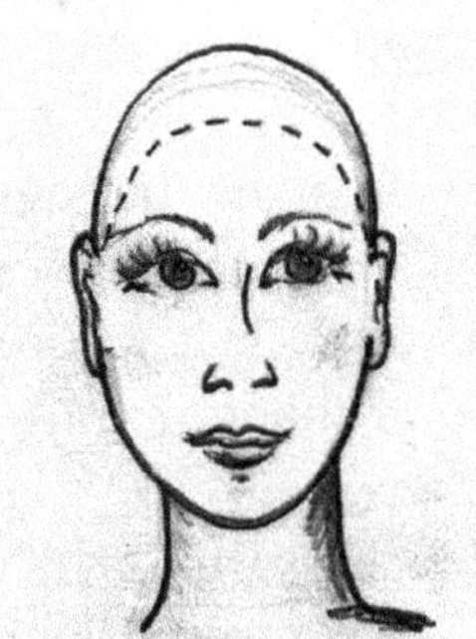

Just make sure that your face stays looking oval once you've finished styling your hair around your face to keep feeling and looking fabulous.

If your face doesn't look oval after you finish styling, tweak the style slightly to create an oval shape again.

ROUND

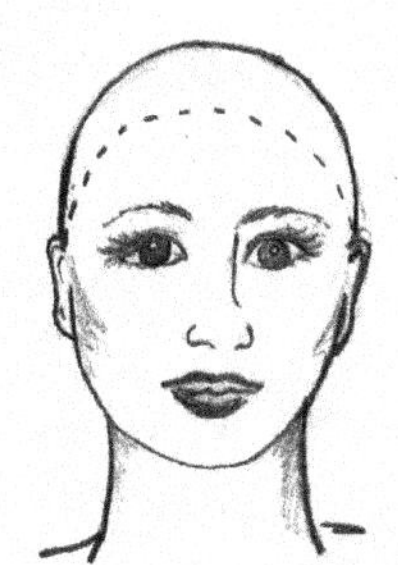

Do: Asymmetrical or longer lengths around the face; or add some height in styling to lengthen round faces. Wear feathered fringes rather than a solid fringe so that your forehead can be seen between the strands of hair.

Don't: Wear your hair flat, wide and chin length. This will widen your face shape and make appear rounder. Full heavy blunt fringes also make your face look wider.

SQUARE

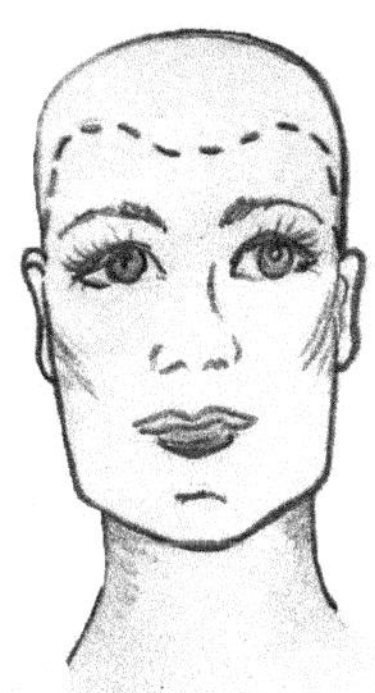

Do: Soften face angles with curls, waves or feathered ends around the face. Square shapes appear more oval on both longer and shorter styles if you do this around the face.

Don't: Pull all of your hair back into a tight ponytail or choose head hugging shapes, as this will emphasize the square-ness of your face.

OBLONG

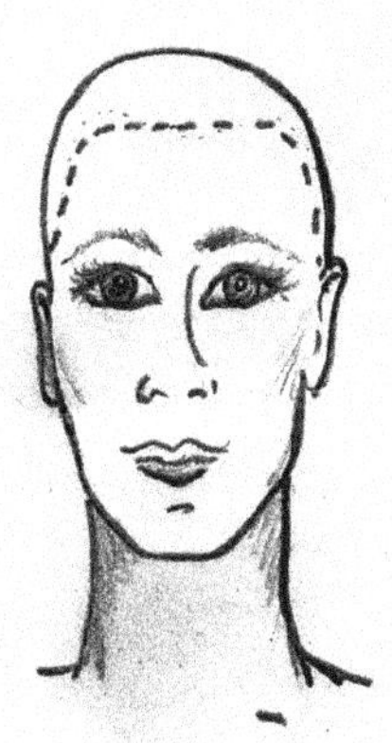

Do: Add fullness at the sides of your face, or wear a fuller fringe or choose jaw length styles to appear more oval than oblong.

Don't: Choose long straight flat styles with no fringe or severe side fringes, or really high styles – it will make your face appear longer than it is.

TRIANGULAR

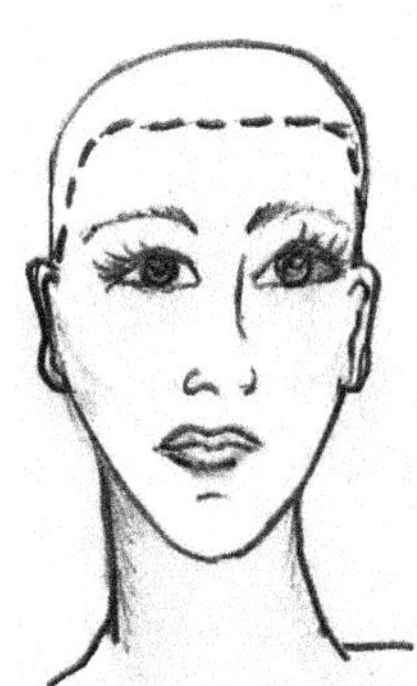

Do: Add fullness around and below the chin area.

Height works with this shape and full fringes that are not too heavy look great.

Don't: Wear short bobs to the earlobe, or wear your hair tightly pulled back – this will emphasize the point of your chin.

HEART

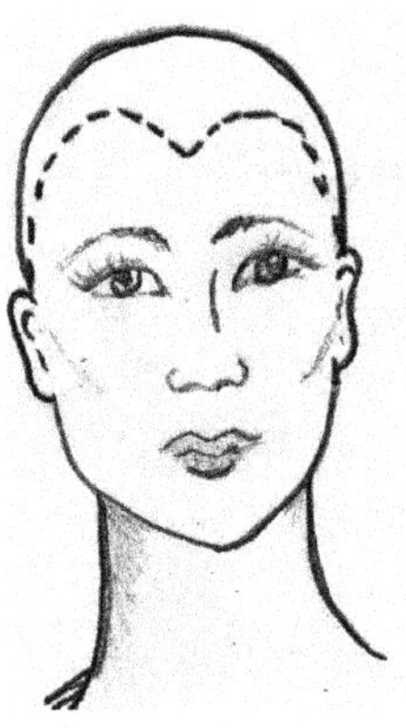

Do: Wear a full fringe, side fringe or curved fringe – hair can be worn any length and will suit this face shape. Seeing the bottom half of the face is almost oval shaped, it's more the width at your forehead that you want to correct.

Don't: Wear a middle part with no fringe, or your hair pulled tightly back off your forehead – it will make your widows peak stand out more.

Can you see the reasons behind knowing your face shape, and how it can benefit you to try and make it appear oval shaped by adjusting your hairstyle?

Try it and see the difference!

All face shapes can usually wear short, medium or long styles. The secret is to adjust your hairstyle to make your face appear more oval shaped and then you will feel happier and more confident about your hair styling every day.

Below I have added examples of different face shapes using the same four styles adjusted slightly so that they still suit the individual face shapes.

OVAL FACE WITH STYLES THAT SUIT OVAL SHAPES

ROUND FACE WITH STYLES THAT SUIT ROUND SHAPES

SQUARE FACE WITH STYLES THAT SUIT SQUARE SHAPES

TRIANGLE FACE WITH STYLES THAT SUIT TRIANGLE SHAPES

OBLONG FACE WITH STYLES THAT SUIT OBLONG SHAPES

HEART FACE WITH STYLES THAT SUIT HEART SHAPES

As you can see above, I chose the same basic four hair styles and adapted them to each different face shape. This was to demonstrate that although you may not have been born with the 'perfect' face shape, you do not have to be limited in style choices.

As long as the style or finish is slightly adjusted to suit your particular face shape, then most styles can look great on you. That is why it is important to know what face shape you have and how to adjust the style so that in your finished hair style your face appears oval.

3. Color Me Fantastic

Do you ever wonder why you choose to wear certain colors and avoid wearing others? I know when I look in my closet I see a lot more of my favorite colors that I love to wear; and none of the colors I don't like.

You may favor wearing a lot of blues, pinks and purples that you feel your best in. Or your favorite colors may be creams, browns, green and oranges and yellow.

It makes a great deal of difference as to how you feel when wearing your favorite colors. Think of how you feel wearing a work uniform in colors that you dislike and wouldn't choose to wear normally.

A friend of mine is naturally very pale skinned with natural ash blonde hair, and her skin is quite pink in the tone. We were talking one day about how she looks wearing anything yellow. After attending three different schools that all had it in their compulsory uniform she was over wearing yellow!

She also feels like wearing yellow drains her face of all color. Yellow also makes her face look more pink than usual. Her natural cool hair tone clashes with the warmth of yellow, making her hair appear to be a dirty unattractive color. The same happens if she wears orange, cream and some browns.

When she wears cool tones to compliment her skin tone like purple or blue, she immediately looks and feels better. This is because cool colors like blue and purple compliment her cool skin tone. The cool colors minimize the redness of her skin, as well as flattering her cool hair color.

Why do you need to know this, and why is it important to think about color?

Because in the same careful way you choose your clothes in fabric tones that suit you and your skin tone; you should also choose your hair colors that work with your skin tone and clothes color choices.

SECRET STYLING TIP #2

Always make sure the colors you choose for your hair will compliment, not clash with your natural skin tone, or general colors of the clothes you favor wearing.

4. Warm and Cool Colors

Which is which? Once you know the answer to this question, it makes it much easier to choose the right colors and tones for your hair that are going to look fantastic on you, and suit you the most.

WARM COLORS:

Red

Orange

Yellow

COOL COLORS:

Blue

Purple

Green

What about the colors that don't fit into the above range of colors like black and brown? If you wear warm colors, you probably choose browns and cream colors to wear and look your best in these colors.

If it's cool colors that you choose to wear, then you may lean towards also wearing black and white, which can suit people with cooler colored skin tones.

Obviously there are many different shades and tones of each color mentioned which can be tricky! The above guide is not a strict one – being aware of whether the colors you choose are cool or warm tones will help in your hair color selection and choices.

Some examples of this are:

With the color red, you could have a cool red or a warm red. Cool reds reflect an undertone of purple in them, or a cherry red feel, whereas warm reds are often a true red, or have an orange undertone.

Purples are cool when they are more of a blue toned purple, but warmer when there is a stronger undertone of red present in the purple shade.

Therefore cool toned skins can look great in a cool red or a soft purple brown, and warm golden toned skins can look great wearing warm toned reds or a reddish purple shade.

Flick through magazines, observe others at your workplace; or even people watch in the supermarket. Take notice of what colors different people are wearing and their hair and skin tone types.

Have they chosen wisely? Do the colors look great and seem to match everything well, or is there something clashing in their color choices that could be improved?

It's interesting to notice how those people who appear more attractive in general wear clothing colors that complement their skin and hair tones. And if their faces appear oval shaped with the design of their hairstyles, then we tend to be more attracted to their total look.

5. Choosing the Right Colors for Your Hair

A lot of my clients leave it up to me to guide them in color choices and I love to come up with amazing complimentary color combinations for each individual.

There are a few things to think about and ask yourself before you can make the right choice. This section is to help you to understand why you love the crazy bright colors on someone else, but would die if a hairdresser gave you the same!

Ask yourself the following questions:

1. Am I an introvert or an extrovert?

This may seem like a strange question, after all we are talking about hair not personality type, so why should it matter?

The reason is that if you are usually a quiet or shy person, you prefer not to draw attention to yourself. Choosing a loud hair color like bright orange with red tips would not make you feel comfortable at all.

On the other hand, if you are more of an outgoing extrovert type, you would hate being given a natural brown color with fine blonde highlights. Color choices which work for you are generally louder, stronger in tone or brighter to match your personality.

2. How regularly am I prepared to visit my hairdresser to keep my color looking great?

This is a great question to ask yourself and to let your hairdresser know the answer. Some choices of color and foils are high maintenance, needing to be re-colored every 3 – 4 weeks.

This can become expensive and time consuming if you are not prepared for the upkeep and can look terrible when you leave it too long between color services.

Other color choices may only need re-coloring every 6 to 8 weeks or longer to maintain the look.

Always check with your hairdresser as to how regularly you will need to come back to keep your color looking at its best.

3. What color clothing do I wear most often?

Choose colors for your hair that compliment your favorite clothes to avoid a color clash.

Remember that if you love to wear pink a lot, being swayed into trying bright orange or red hair could be a bad choice for you, unless you are an extrovert who loves drawing attention with bright clashing colors.

4. How long do I want the color to last?

Sometimes you just want a little color to highlight or add richness in your hair for a particular event or party. Other times you want your color to be an ongoing change and to last as long as possible. Ask your hairdresser what short term options there are, like semi-permanent colors or individual colored hair extensions.

I often hear from clients that they would like two or three colors but they aren't sure what will work together in their hair.

Because there are so many shades of every color available, I have written up a simple guide to help you with the color choice process. Next time you visit your salon you will be able to make better choices to suit your skin tone and clothing choices.

GUIDE TO GREAT COLOR CHOICES FOR YOUR SKIN TYPE

COOL SKIN	*Introverted Personality*	- Ash brown/blonde, cool toned blondes - Violet toned browns or blondes - Cool subtle reds and red browns - Mahogany browns, plum tones
	Extroverted Personality	- Cool blue black - Deep reds, purple browns - Bright reds and purples - Bleach/very light blondes with cool tones - Ash, silver, purple or rose tones on blondes
WARM SKIN	*Introverted Personality*	- Golden browns and blondes - Blonde and brown shades with a beige tone - Copper browns, auburn tones - Strawberry blonde/ copper blondes - Subtle copper reds
	Extroverted Personality	- Bright true reds or vibrant coppers - Black with red undertones - Warm browns with dramatic highlights - Splices of contrast color/s - Bleach/very light blondes with cool tones - Beige, gold, copper or strawberry blonde tones

Final Color Tips to remember:

- Cool colors + Cool skin = Best combination.
- Warm colors + Warm skin = Best combination.
- *Introverted personalities* love and feel more comfortable with more natural and subtle tones when coloring their hair.
- *Extroverted personalities* love brighter, stronger panels of colors and tones on themselves when choosing colors for their hair.
- If your eyes are warm (blue, brown or hazel) and your skin is a cool color, then both warm and cool colors can look great on you.
- If your eyes are cool (green or gray) and your skin is a warm color, then you too can wear both cool and warm hair colors.

6. Product Mania

Imagine yourself at the supermarket or in a salon trying to find the right product to make your hair look healthy and amazing.

In front of you is every color, shape, size and type of products – all vying for your attention on the shelves. There are so many to choose from that you may end up just picking the most attractive bottle or what seems to be the best value for money. Sometimes we leave with the wrong product; or give up because it is too hard to decide and leave with none at all!

Can you believe that in the Eighties there were only four main types of products to choose from?

Well it's true! Back then there was only a choice of hairspray, gel, mousse and setting lotion. That seems unbelievable doesn't it!

With the glut of products now available on the market these days, it's very hard to imagine. Back then there were only a few product types around to confuse us, instead of hundreds.

When I was a young girl who loved playing with hair, I noticed a new advertisement on the television for a wonderful new product that was taking the world by storm – mousse!! The white fluffy foam expanded like magic on the screen, and I was enthralled.

I recall thinking how cool it looked, and hoping my mother would get some so I could try it! I thought mousse was incredibly amazing and exciting at the time.

Now it's laughable as you think of the hundreds of products currently available on the shelves. The thought of being excited when a new hair product is launched is totally foreign to us now.

These days more new products on the supermarket and salon shelves almost make us cringe – another one to add to the list of products out there that you don't know what to do with!

A lot of us buy products we have seen advertised because we think they sound great and will fix the problem. It also looks appealing on the shelf, and we are excited to get home and try our newly purchased product.

We are often disappointed with the result in our hair. The product excitedly chosen either doesn't have enough hold, it's too sticky, or makes your hair flat and greasy and doesn't measure up to the claims made on television.

Discouraged, you give it at least a few tries in case it was your styling technique that didn't work. Eventually you are finally convinced the product is totally wrong for your hair. So you shove the offending product into the back of the bathroom cupboard. It joins all of the other products that also sounded great when advertised, but simply didn't get the results you were expecting in your hair.

The problem then is the full cupboard of hair products wasting space that you don't really want to throw out because they were so expensive when you bought them.

What my aim is in this section, is to make it easier for you to choose a product type that will best suit your own hair length, type and style, so that you're not adding any more dud products to the rejected pile of products shoved in the back of a cupboard!

I have added instructions for product usage and the lengths and hair types that each product works best with, and how or where to apply each styling product.

BASIC GUIDE TO STYLING PRODUCT TYPES AVAILABLE

PRODUCT TYPE	PRODUCT STRENGTH	HAIR LENGTH/ TYPE	HOW TO USE IT
Hairspray	Light/ Medium	Short/ Medium/ Long All Hair Types	Hold can 20 – 30cms from hair and lightly mist over finished style

PRODUCT TYPE	PRODUCT STRENGTH	HAIR LENGTH/ TYPE	HOW TO USE IT
Lacquer	Strong/Extra Strong	Short/ Medium/Long Fine / Medium Hair	Hold can 20 – 30cms from hair and spray over the top of finished style – don't use too much as these sprays are strong
Mousse	Medium/ Strong	Short/ Medium Hair All Hair Types	Egg size dollop on hand, distribute to both hands, apply to roots for extra lift, or mid-ends for all over hold before drying hair
Gel	Medium/ Strong	Short/ Medium Hair All Hair Types	Can use on wet or dry hair, spread through small amount with fingers. The look achieved with gel is a wet look
Root Lift Spray	Medium	Short/ Medium/Long Fine Hair	Lift hair and spray directly at root areas to give more body to your hair when wet then blow dry and style
Shine Spray	Light/None	Medium/Long Hair All Hair Types	Mist into the air high in front of you, step under mist with styled hair for instant shine. On a non-washing day, spray lightly on dry looking frizzy or fluffy ends to add shine and control fluffiness. Great to mist over up-styles too.
Shine Drops	Light/None	Medium/Long Hair All Hair Types	Spread small amount on fingers, apply to ends of hair mainly, and very lightly only on mid lengths/ top of head after styling
Wax	Light/ Medium	Short/ Medium Hair All Hair Types	Spread small amount onto your fingertips on dry hair, warm by rubbing together then apply mainly to root area in a circular motion
Paste	Medium/ Strong	Short/ Medium Hair Fine/Medium Hair	Small amount spread on hands first on wet or dry hair & work through hair roots to ends & style
Anti-Frizz Serum	Light/None	Medium/Long Hair Medium/Coarse Hair	After styling, apply to mid-lengths and ends only first, then *lightly* at the top if frizzy there too. If you use too much your hair can appear greasy
Leave-in Moisturiser	None	Medium/Long Hair All Hair Types	Use a 10 -20 cent piece on palm, spread through mid-lengths to the ends of hair. Best applied to wet hair before styling to help control frizz and dryness

PRODUCT TYPE	PRODUCT STRENGTH	HAIR LENGTH/ TYPE	HOW TO USE IT
Thermal Spray	Light/None to Medium/ Strong	Short/ Medium/ Long All Hair Types	Protects hair from heat damage. Spray on wet or dry hair before using heat tool to protect hair. When straightening or curling, lightly mist over each dry section
Styling Paste	Medium/ Strong	Short/ Medium Hair Fine/Medium Hair	Work a small amount through wet or dry hair from roots to tips
Mud	Strong/Extra Strong	Short Hair Fine/Medium Hair	Warm the mud with hands first by rubbing it between your fingers. Aim to apply first to the roots of dry hair, then through to the ends
Clay	Extra Strong	Short Hair Fine/Medium Hair	Use a small amount of this stronger product for dull grunge look, can also make finer hair appear thicker. Sometimes better applied on wet hair as it can be harder to spread through dry hair
Argan Oil	No Hold	Medium/Long All Hair Types	Argan oil adds shine and moisture to the hair, and tames frizziness. Apply sparingly to the mid-lengths and ends. The most popular brand is Moroccanoil.

As you can see there are a wide variety of products on the market that can achieve many different results and work better with different lengths of hair. This chart will be helpful in making good choices for your hair and styling will be easier with the right products.

Remember that if you are buying your styling products from a salon, the product is more concentrated. For example super strength gel from your hairdresser is going to be much stronger than super strength gel from the supermarkets, but is usually more expensive too. However you use less of the product each time you style, and you get the result you want.

When buying styling products from a salon, you have the added advantage of advice from a professional who can see your hair and the style. You are more likely to buy a styling product that works best for what you want to achieve style wise.

If you can choose the right products to fit your hair's particular styling needs, then you are half way there to being able to create great hair yourself!

7. Supermarket Versus Salon

There are so many products available both on the supermarket and salon shelves. Unbelievably they all profess to be different, so that gives us thousands of products to choose from. *No wonder we are all confused!*

I want to address the age old question of "Which is better - salon products or supermarket products - and why?"

Being a hairdresser you may assume I will just tell you that salon products are much better every time but this is not *always* the case!

There is no simple answer for this question, as it depends on each person's hair and the type of hair you are referring to for each individual.

If you are looking for a shampoo and conditioner for a child's hair the considerations before selecting a product are:

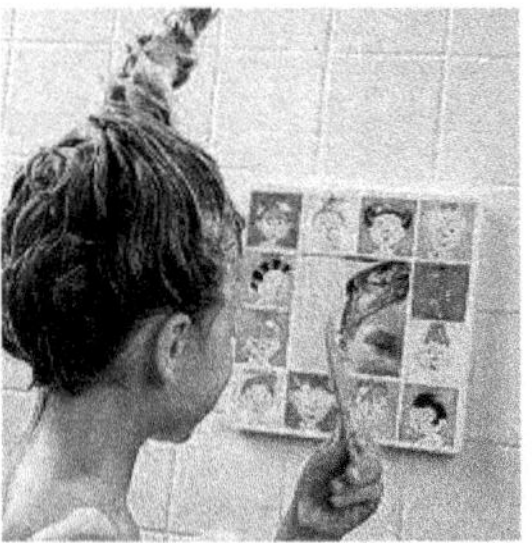

- Children's hair is usually natural with no colors or perm.
- They don't dry out their hair using hot styling tools
- Their hair is often in good condition. (unless they often swim in chlorinated pools)
- When shampooing their own hair, they are likely to use large quantity of product each time
- Kids can easily waste a large amount of shampoo and conditioner over time

Considering the points above, probably the best choice for children could be the cheaper mild shampoos and conditioners specifically for children available in the supermarkets.

However if your child does swim regularly in chlorinated pools consider using salon products that can remove the damaging chlorine from hair. If you ever use your hot styling tool on their hair, protect your child's hair with a heat protectant spray first which can minimize loss of moisture and damage to hair.

If you are looking for a shampoo and conditioner for an adult who has natural hair in good condition and wears it in a short style; then either salon or supermarket product choice could work.

If your hair is colored, bleached, permed or sun damaged you're best to choose a professional salon product and utilize the stylists knowledge to choose the products which will work best in your hair. Even if your hair is not colored, chemically straightened or permed; hot styling tools, the sun and air conditioning can damage your hair more than you'd imagine.

I recommend using salon prescribed products to get the best results for your hair. Ask your stylist for the best shampoo and conditioner for your hair condition and type and they will be thrilled to assist you.

SECRET STYLING TIP #3

To achieve the best results possible always ask your hairdresser to recommend the best shampoo, conditioner or styling product for your particular hair needs.

Some great salons will give you a small sample to try for free, so you can see how it works in your hair before you buy the product. Some brand ranges are also available to purchase in a mini size too which is helpful in testing the product on your hair.

To give you more guidance on the differences between supermarket and salon products, I have outlined general features, benefits and negatives to help make it easier for you to choose the right product for your hair.

Supermarket Products

- Usually not as strong or concentrated as salon products
- Shampoos and conditioners have a higher percentage of water content than the salon brands
- Products appear cheaper and better value
- Advertised on TV as miraculous but often disappointing
- Styling products often are weaker in strength and hold so you are forced to use a lot more each time
- Packaged in containers that appear larger so you think you're getting a bargain
- Ingredients may be cheaper synthetic ingredients
- Products used up faster because more is needed and used each time
- Have to choose products yourself with no professional help available

Salon Products

- More concentrated products so less amount needed each time
- Smaller sizes (especially shampoo and conditioner) that last longer than larger bottles when correct amount is used
- Better results when styling daily because good hair condition is maintained
- More expensive so can appear to be less value for money
- Correct product choice can control frizz, strengthen hair, increase longevity of color tone and improve condition and manageability of your hair
- Benefit of professionals for advice and recommending the correct products for your hair needs
- Trend towards more natural ingredients used in salon products – many are now sulfate free and paraben free

- Scientific teams research effects and benefits of ingredients to create individual products to suit different hair types and needs
- Incorrect product choices for your hair type and condition can be an expensive mistake

Looking at the above comparisons and points, there seems to be some positives and negatives in both choices.

To truly be able to choose the best products for you to help you to manage your hair, we need further comparisons based on reasons why we choose to buy a particular product.

Size and Cost

Let's face it; a lot of us choose products based on price alone. So let's have a look at salon shampoos and conditioners versus their supermarket counterparts and compare them.

Salon: 300mls each @ $25 each = **Cost:** $50 for 600mls product.

Supermarket: 500mls each @ $10 each = **Cost:** $20 for 1000mls product.

So far if choice is made on price alone, everyone would choose the supermarket shampoo and conditioner. After all, the price of the salon products does seem to be five times more expensive than the supermarket products.

But we base our choice of shampoo and conditioner purchase on more reasons than price alone. What else do we want to consider other than the price?

Quantity of Product Used

There is definitely a big difference in the quantity you would need to use of salon and supermarket products. This is worth emphasizing! Because the salon products are so concentrated you only need to use a small amount each time. Supermarket shampoos and conditioners are not as concentrated, so to get the product to work effectively you need to use more each time.

Consider the following:

Salon shampoo and conditioner: 600mls: A 10 - 20 cent piece in the palm (5mls).

2 x shampoos + 1 x conditioner = 15mls used each time.

So out of our 600mls of shampoo and conditioner costing $50.00, you would get 40 uses = $1.25 each.

Supermarket shampoo and conditioner, 1000mls: A palm full used each application (12mls).

2 x shampoos + 1 x conditioner = 36mls used each time.

So out of our 1000mls of shampoo and conditioner, you would get 27 uses = $0.74 each.

When you look at the comparison of amounts used, you can see that the price difference is actually not that big per use. If the correct amounts are used each time, the price difference is now less than half, with there being 51 cents difference in cost per use.

The number of uses you get with each product are different though – 40 hair washes out of the salon product, and only 27 washes out of the supermarket products.

This means another supermarket trip to purchase more supermarket shampoo and conditioner and using it another 13 times before the original salon shampoo and conditioner is empty.

Therefore in consideration of amount used and costs:

40 hair washes with salon products = $50

40 hair washes with supermarket products = $29.60

This shows now that in comparison there is now closer to only $20 in cost between them, instead of $30.

We also went from the salon product looking like it was five times more expensive than supermarket products; to them being much closer in value. With the generic example I have given, salon products are only 1.7 times more expensive than supermarket brands when the correct amount is used each time.

Visible Results

Another deciding factor when choosing what products to buy for our hair is *results*. If the shampoo and conditioner promises to stop color fade, or make your hair frizz free or make it stronger, then that's what you want to see.

It's exciting buying a new product to try. You see it advertised and the model's hair looking fantastic and think yes, that's what I need! But when you get it home and use it for a while you realize that it doesn't work as they promised on the television and you are disappointed with the results.

The reason the models' hair looked fantastic is probably not the shampoo she was advertising. It was more likely the professional stylists that the shampoo company hired - with their professional shine sprays, products and tools as well as years of expertise that made the models hair look fabulous for the advertisement.

Salon shampoo and conditioner is usually developed by a team of scientists, and tailored to specific hair types and problems. If you are recommended the correct salon shampoo and conditioner for your hair type and problem, you can achieve excellent results every day. They also create specific products designed to maintain color brightness and longevity so your color looks great for longer.

Supermarket shampoos and conditioners can be disappointing in results. Even if you have chosen the correct shampoo and conditioner for your particular hair type, results can still be less than satisfactory. Almost all supermarket shampoos contain sodium laurel sulfate.

The chemical compounds in the sulfates dehydrate the sebaceous (oil) glands and strip your scalp of essential oils and natural moisture.

These compounds also tend to damage the hair follicles, which can lead to hair loss.

In summary, there are a lot of factors to consider when you buy products. The best thing to do is to do a basic assessment of your own hair first. Ask yourself the following:

- Is my hair damaged and dry from color, perming, straightening, blow drying or any other reason?
- Is my hair natural and in good condition?
- Is there any frizz, dryness or natural curl that I can't control in my hair?

If you feel that you have specific problems that drive you crazy and are difficult for you to fix, then going to the salon for a professional recommendation for the right products for your hair type or problem would be more beneficial.

This will make it easier for you to choose the right products for your hair so you can look fabulous every day, and to fix specific hair problems.

The only caution I would give you when you have wonderful salon products for your hair is to protect them from the rest of your family. Why do I say this? Because expensive shampoo and conditioner can be wasted, without you realizing it!

Take the example of Corinne, a friend of mine who had a fabulous new color done, and decided to splash out on shampoo and conditioner. She bought some expensive color shampoo and conditioner from the salon which cost her around $50 at the time. Corinne loved the shampoo and conditioner, her color was staying rich and glossy, and she couldn't believe how little she needed to use each time.

That was until her husband got hold of it!

You may think "So what? He's probably only got short hair, how much could he use?" Her husband shaves his head, so he has no hair at all; so it wasn't himself he wasted it on.

Corinne came home one day to find that her husband had decided the dog needed a wash. He had searched around, but couldn't find the dog shampoo. Thinking, that 'hair was hair' he figured it wouldn't matter if he used the shampoo from their bathroom.

Next thing you know, the bottle was half empty, the dog smelt and looked wonderful, and her color was unlikely to fade; but there was two *very* unhappy owners standing over her.

Her husband had no idea of how much the shampoo had cost but I can guarantee he will never do that again!

Husbands and boyfriends are not the only prospective product wasters.

If you have children that can reach your shampoos to tip them all over the floor or teenagers that use handfuls each time, then leaving expensive products in the bathroom is not advisable if you are after value for money!

Unless they have a specific hair problem, buy them their own cheaper versions to keep in the shower and protect your expensive salon products that were prescribed specifically for your hair by taking them to the bathroom only when you are about to use them.

8. Mastering the Hot Stuff

There is a plethora of hot styling tools available on the market today. Finding the right ones for your hair and styling abilities can be difficult.

Some of them (if used incorrectly) can actually burn your hair to the point of it breaking off, so it's good to have a guide on the uses of hot tools and how to be cautious of when using hot tools on your fragile hair.

Many people think hair is quite strong and it can appear to be, but everyone knows what happens when you hold a flame near any hair – it burns and shrivels up very quickly, not to mention the horrible smell of the hair burning.

Let's start with a list of types of hot tools.

The most popular hot styling tools available on the market today are:

- Blow drier
- Straightening iron
- Curling tongs
- Conical wand
- Hot rollers
- Crimpers
- Triple barrel tongs

You might own and use one or more of the above hot styling tools. You may even use more than one of these tools each day on your hair. Perhaps you don't own any of the above styling tools, but would like to buy one of them.

If you are unsure as to which one you will be able to use, or what would work on your hair, the following information will be helpful for you.

One of the most important styling tips to help keep your hair looking beautiful for longer is this:-

SECRET STYLING TIP #4

When using a hot styling tool on your hair, always allow your hair to cool down completely before styling, brushing or running your fingers through your dry hair, to ensure a longer lasting hair style."

If your hair is still hot following the use of a hot styling tool and you run your fingers through it or brush it, your style will drop out faster. If you want lots of body to stay on your blow dry, your curls to stay bouncy or your freshly straightened hair to stay straight and frizz free; wait until your hair has cooled down before you touch it.

Have you ever wondered why there is a cool shot button on your hairdryer?

Perhaps you have thought it seems like a silly setting to have, because who would want to dry their hair with cold air? Surely it takes much longer to dry hair with cold air and is much faster to dry hair with warm or hot air?

The cool shot button is great to use as you finish drying each section of hair with hot air. Once the section is dry, if you give your hair a shot of cold air for a few seconds, it will make the style hold for much longer and will keep more lift in the root area of your hair for longer. It ensures your hair will stay where you want it with extra volume, smoothness or curl than if you had not left it to cool down.

The following is a summary of what the different hot styling tools are great for and why you need to be careful when using them.

Blow Driers

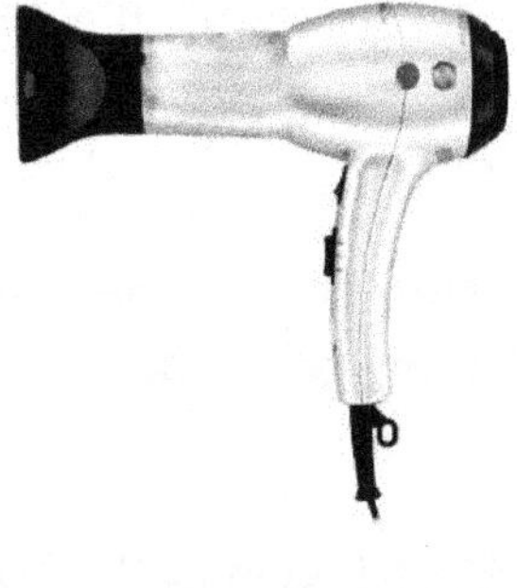

Great for:

- Quick drying of wet hair
- Achieving body and volume into the roots of your hair
- Styling with a round brush or vent brush
- Controlling stubborn cowlicks and crazy crown growths when you dry them first and direct the strong root growth to where you would prefer it to sit (make sure you hold it firmly into place and give it a cool shot it after drying too)

Be careful of:

- Holding the drier in one place on your head for too long and burning your scalp
- High heat that can fry your hair in an instant and cause long lasting damage
- Small round brushes on medium to long hair can get caught and tangled easily

Straightening Irons

Great for:

- Fixing kinks in your hair on a 'non hair washing' day
- Straightening curly or frizzy hair easily
- Smoothing away the fluffy flyaway rogue hairs
- Curling or waving dry hair

Be careful of:

- Keeping the irons on one section of hair for too long – the irons are often over 200 degrees Celsius (or 392 degrees Fahrenheit) and hair is fragile – it can frizz then break off with high heat on it for too long
- Using straighteners near your ears, forehead and neck – it only takes a second to create a nasty burn on your skin
- Being aware of the surface that you rest your hot irons on in between use – don't put them down near any water or rest them on a plastic bench or surface that could be damaged by the heat of your straightening iron

Curling Tongs and Conical Wands

Great for:

- Creating soft or bouncy spiral curls
- Different barrel sizes can give different size curls and different looks
- Adding curls to a casual up style
- Changing your day look to an evening out look
- Creating soft waves

Be careful of:

- The fine ends of your hair can miss being curled and you end up with straight ends
- The ends going frizzy when they're not secured smoothly around the barrel
- Disturbing your curls when hair is still hot – it will drop the curls out faster
- Burning your fingers when winding your hair onto the conical wand (a heat protectant glove is recommended)
- Leaving your hair wound up in the tongs for too long – you can irreversibly damage or burn your hair

Hot Rollers

Great for:

- Adding body, curl and root lift to style dry hair
- Style support for up-styles like French rolls
- Getting soft to medium curls all over quite quickly
- Adding height on the crown area of your head

Be careful of:

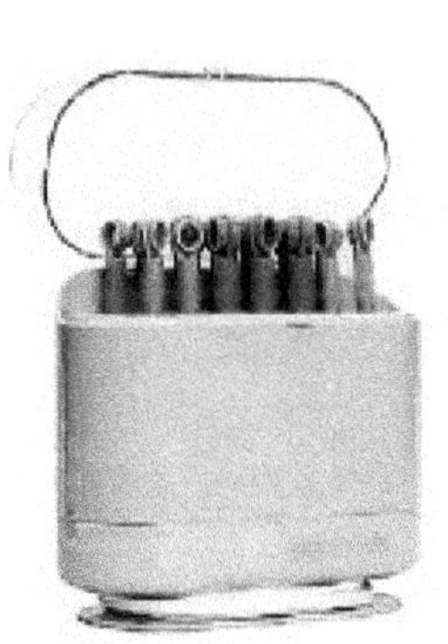

- Burning your fingers if you aren't fast enough when rolling your hair onto the rollers – they get really hot
- Not getting the ends of the hair onto the roller smoothly- it causes hair to come out frizzy
- Hot rollers near your ears and neck can burn – wedge a tissue or some cotton wool between your ear or neck and the roller to protect your skin from being burnt
- Wait until hair is cool to style – if the hair is still warm when styling the curl result will become much softer or can drop out

Crimpers and Triple Barrel Tongs

Great for:

- Adding quirky pieces to your hairstyle
- Party styling
- Crimped pieces in funky up styles
- Triple barrels give a great soft wave in medium and long hair

Be careful of:

- Not matching the crimps or waves up properly on your hair and ending up with strange indents in your style
- Leaving the tongs or crimpers on the same section of your hair for too long, as it can permanently damage your hair
- Skin burns when working near your ears or neck area

As you can see, all of these hot styling tools have the potential to do some real damage to your hair. One of the most important things to remember when using all of the above hot styling tools is this:

SECRET STYLING TIP #5

When styling your hair with any hot styling tool protect your hair from moisture loss and use a protective heat shield spray on your hair first. This will help ensure your hair doesn't lose too much of its natural moisture and prevent mechanical damage to your hair.

What should you use? What is mechanical damage? And what differences will it make?

Mechanical damage is the term professional's use when presented with hair that has been damaged from hot styling tools.

With mechanical damage from blow drying or using a straightening iron, your hair can appear frizzy in odd places, some hair could even be broken and some sections of hair can be difficult to manage and 'grab' onto your brush when styling.

There are many products available that have a heat protectant in them, or that have been created solely to protect your hair from heat damage. It's like putting on sunscreen for your skin.

If you were to spend a few hours in the full sun these days, you would apply sunscreen to your skin before heading outside, to prevent it being burnt and damaged by the sun's heat.

The thermo (heat) protecting products for your hair do the same kind of thing. They form a protective film over your hair, sealing in your natural moisture to help keep your hair in great condition.

You can get some heat shield products with different strengths of styling hold, some that also have shine or leave in moisture incorporated into the product and others are protective heat shields only. It's worth shopping around to find one that feels right on your hair and achieves the result you want for your style.

9. Finding a New Stylist

One of the most difficult things to do is to find a great new hairdresser.

This is especially true when you move to a new area, or if your favorite hairdresser suddenly disappears from the salon you like to go to.

A friend of mine told me about her cousin Julie who had moved from Melbourne to Sydney over twelve months ago. Although she loved her new life in Sydney, there was one small problem... her hair.

Julie decided that she needed to find a new hairdresser. She tried looking for one in her new neighborhood first. After being disappointed by all three different salons was at her wits end with a horrible haircut!

None of the salons felt comfortable. One stylist was rude. Another didn't listen to what she wanted and the last stylist didn't seem to care whether Julie was happy or not with her hairstyle.

Julie decided to increase the frequency of her visits back home to Melbourne. At least her old favorite hairdresser knew her hair well, knew what she liked and always did a fantastic job.

She has been flying between states for two years and although inconvenient, feels it is worth it for her because she loves her hair again now.

You may wonder how extreme or common is flying interstate for hair appointments?

Some of you are thinking *surely* she could have found a good one in her new neighborhood!

Others are nodding in agreement and understand totally! Some women are happy to travel a good distance to see their preferred stylist every time too.

Finding a new hairdresser can be daunting. That's why so many people tend to stick with the one they know and trust, rather than having to chance someone new, even if they have to travel a long way to remain loyal. This could be very inconvenient, expensive in time, and difficult to maintain depending on your circumstances.

If you are happy to make the trip to your regular favorite stylist whether it is across town or interstate then that's great! I'm sure your stylist appreciates the distance you travel to see them and your loyalty.

Sometimes however, that is not a feasible option.

The Disappearing Stylist

At times, your favorite hairdresser disappears off the face of the earth, never to be found again. Often without warning! It could be a change in job, career, motherhood, location or a health or physical reason for their disappearance.

When a hairstylist informs their employer that they are leaving to go to a new position, they would usually give a week or two of notice to the employer.

However the employer may choose to decline the notice and ask them to finish up immediately. Some salon owners prefer to pay the stylist for the notice given rather than allow them to continue working in the salon.

This is because the employer has worked hard to build up their business. If they allow the hairdresser that's leaving two more weeks to work in the salon, the stylist may inform the clients where she is going and the salon's owner will lose their business.

This practice may seem unfair to those of you who have lost a great hairdresser in this way. At least you know it wasn't that your stylist didn't care about you, and probably did want to say goodbye to you. It's much more likely that the stylist was not allowed to, and client records and information remains the property of the salon, not individual stylists.

It is also understandable from a business owner's point of view that they have put a lot of money and effort into growing their business and must protect their asset and client base.

There are a high percentage of women in the industry, and a common reason for them leaving is pregnancy. A lot of people I know have lost their preferred stylist to motherhood. Sometimes this is for a short period, other times the stylist never returns to salon work.

Another way you may have lost your favorite stylist (and a very common reason for giving up the hairdressing profession) is physical problems. Standing all day, bending over squirming children and having to bend yourself into all sorts of positions day in and day out can cause many physical problems.

The areas affected the most for hairdressers are feet, legs, shoulders, neck, back and hands. Work related problems can result in an increase of varicose veins, swelling of ankles, inflammation throughout the body, carpel tunnel and require all sorts of operations we'd prefer not to have.

I know of several ex hair stylists who have had carpel tunnel surgery on their hands and shoulder operations as a result of repetitive movements related to the profession. Most stylists who have worked in the industry long term have issues with their backs.

No matter what the reason, sometimes you find yourself without a favorite hairdresser and at some point in your life and need to find yourself a new one!

For those times I want to give you some tips on how you can successfully find yourself a wonderful new stylist who will listen to you and create a fantastic style you will love every time.

When you are looking for a new hairdresser consider the following suggestions to make your search a little easier.

Recommendations

Do you have a friend whose hair you always admire? Then ask your friend which salon they go to as well as the name of the stylist that created their style for them. They will be pleased that you noticed, and happy to share that information with you.

If you are new to an area and don't know anyone there that can recommend a stylist to you, this can still work. Visit the local shopping district and observe local shoppers there for a style or color that you think is spectacular and really well cut.

Once you have spotted someone whose hair you admire, approach them in a friendly way. Tell them how wonderful their hair looks, and ask who their hairdresser is; you are bound to get a positive response every time!

I have gained quite a few new clients who have to come to me personally over the years, because they had seen and loved one of my client's hairstyles or colors. My clients have been approached by these strangers often in the street and asked who did their hair. I find it's a great compliment for me as a hairstylist when this happens.

People are usually delighted to receive such a compliment from a stranger and are more than happy to share the secret of where they got their hair done and who was the stylist. They may even have a business card from the salon with them that they can give you!

With technology today we don't even need a card or to write the information down – we can immediately search the internet for the business recommended and save the information.

Online recommendations (such as Google reviews, salons Facebook pages or Trip Advisor) are also helpful. Reviews posted independently by clients with pictures are the best to give you an idea of whether you think the stylists work is what you are looking for.

SECRET STYLING TIP #6

When searching for a new hairdresser, either approach someone that you think has a fantastic style cut or color and ask them where they got it done and who was their stylist, or search online for local salons and stylists who are recommended with pictures.

I have not mentioned any advertising fliers or adverts in the newspapers or magazines as a way of finding a new salon and stylist as yet.

That's because I believe that starting with a recommendation from someone who has been to the salon and has great hair should be your first choice. You then get to see an example of the work done by the stylist first. Social media is another great way to view stylist's work. Many salons post clients' before and after pictures via social media sites like Facebook or Instagram, or on the salon's website.

If you receive an offer in the post, or see something advertised that would work for you, definitely check out the salon and the offer if you feel it's the right thing for you.

There are a few more tips to help make the hunt for a new hairdresser easier for you though, which will also help when you receive an offer from a salon you'd like to try.

Check Out the Salon First

The reason I think it's a good idea to go and have a look at the salon you have been recommended to go to, or have an offer from is to find out whether you will feel comfortable going in there or not.

There are so many different types of salons, and not all of them will suit you.

Some salons have a young funky feel, others are clinical and bare with an intimidating feel. Other salons are stuck in the eighties and have not changed their décor, or have music pumping out of them loudly.

Some salons are in a very busy shopping center or district with open areas, exposing foiled clients to the stares and scrutiny of the passing public. Some are located in areas where parking is an issue.

There are some that also seem unprofessional and unfriendly, with bored gum chewing stylists who seem more interested in doing their own hair rather than bothering with doing yours.

Thankfully some salons are beautifully presented with a positive feel to them. Friendly, professional stylists who greet you with a welcoming smile when you arrive are a must!

What you want to find in a salon is something that matches you and your hair. You want to feel comfortable, welcomed and relaxed no matter what the décor or location.

If you want to have a really good look at a salon without drawing strange looks, walk by after hours when they are closed to check it out and see if it is somewhere you would feel comfortable.

Ask Questions

Once you have had a recommendation from someone and checked out the salon, you want to make sure it's somewhere you will like visiting when you need to talk to a stylist about your hair.

Many great salons and stylists will offer you a free consultation, without the obligation of an appointment.

Even if it is only a few minutes that the stylist has to chat to you, it will still give you a good idea whether you would like to entrust your precious hair to the stylist.

Consultations are a great time to ask questions of your stylist, so be prepared with an idea of what you want to know and ask away!

Some of the questions you may ask could include:

- How much experience have they had
- How long will the color/style take to do

- What will be the cost
- How often will I have to maintain the style
- What do they think will suit you and why
- Can they create the style you would like

A great stylist is always happy to take a few minutes to chat to you about your hair, especially when you are a prospective new client to their salon.

If the salon you have chosen to visit does not allow their stylists to spend a few minutes chatting to you about your hair, or if they seem uninterested or perhaps answer your questions poorly, then that could be an indication that that particular salon is not right for you.

Always Bring Pictures

"A picture paints a thousand words."

Nothing is truer than that statement when it comes to your hair. You can experience immense difficulties in expressing your style ideas to a stylist who may use different terms to describe things, or choose different language to you.

Pictures of styles and colors can immediately give the stylist a starting point.

SECRET STYLING TIP #7

"When you bring in pictures of a cut or color you love and want, you have a much better chance of the hairstylist understanding what you like rather than just trying to explain it to them in words alone."

For example, if you ask for a short haircut around the neck and ears, with a longer side fringe, you may think you are giving a thorough easy explanation of what style you would like. However, this is often not the case. Have a look at the example pictures I have added in here to illustrate my point.

You can see that they all fit the basic description of short at sides and back, with a longer side fringe, but they all look *completely* different.

Obviously we are not all going to look exactly like the person that is in the picture.

Your face shape may be different, or the texture of your hair may be fine and lank, whereas the model in the picture may have thick coarser textured hair than you. Perhaps your hair is naturally straight, and the model's hair is naturally curly.

Ask yourself and the stylist whether the style will suit your face shape.

That's the reason why my picture suggestion is so helpful to the stylist. It is especially helpful when visiting a salon for the first time and when you want a style or color change.

It makes communicating the style you would like much easier on you – you don't have to find the right words to describe the style or color tones you like, instead exactly what you want is easily described with looking at the right picture.

Maybe it is the hair colors and tones you would like replicated on your hair from the picture. Ask yourself and the stylist whether it will suit your skin tone and eye color.

The answers to these questions are easy when the stylist has a clear picture in front of them with what you would like them to achieve.

They can then tell you if the style and or colors are possible, or whether a slight adjustment to suit your hair type, face shape or skin tones would suit you better and why.

Of course some clients have unrealistic expectations.

They bring in a picture of a model in her twenties when they themselves are in their fifties, and expect to look the same as their picture when they walk out the salon door.

Unfortunately even the very best of the best stylists would struggle to achieve that, being as it would be impossible unless they were also booked in for cosmetic surgery later that afternoon!

What I am trying to say is to be realistic in your ideas and expectations of what a stylist can create and achieve with your particular hair type and color.

I have actually had quite a few clients that request that I transform them from fifty-something to twenty something while I am consulting with them, but luckily I know they are joking when they ask if I can get the face the same as the picture as well!

I would love to be able to say "Yes, sure, no problems at all! I can have it all done for you in less than two hours, the twenty year old face included!"

Unfortunately hair stylists were only given scissors and hair tools to work with not a magic wand... Though we all wish we could have one of those at times!

As a stylist myself though, I love it when clients bring in pictures for me. It gives me a great starting point, shows me what my client would like to achieve, and also what type of finish and style is attractive to them. (Whether it is a traditional style, funky, retro, sleek or messy finish etc.)

I definitely think it is a great idea for both client and stylist, and encourages better consultations. Many clients that have been unhappy with their haircuts, styles or colors that did not bring in a picture, could have possibly avoided being given a style that they didn't like.

Of course not all people who bring in a picture (or sometimes five) have chosen one that will suit their face shape and not all hairdressers may have the skill or time to create the look in the pictures.

It is up to the hairstylist to help you look your best, so they should be telling you if they don't think that the style or color will suit you, and most importantly *WHY* they think that.

Maybe the style is almost right, but would suit your face shape better if it was slightly longer or shorter, or perhaps more layered and feathered around your face or at the sides above your ears.

A slight adjustment to the style you have chosen could be all it needs to make it a great choice for your hair and look fantastic.

If you have not thought to bring along a picture to the salon, or remember that the picture you were going to bring to show the stylist is still pinned to the fridge door at home, don't worry!

Most of the salons around have hair style books for you to look through and it's a good idea if you are able to arrive a few minutes early for your appointment. When you arrive, ask the stylist that greets you for some style books to have a look at and mark a few pictures you like as you find them, ready to show your stylist in consultation.

Whatever it is that you would like to have done to your hair, whether it be a color or three colors, a change in hair cut or just a different fringe, bringing in a picture will get you closer to the achieving the hair you would love to have!

The Stylist

Finding the right stylist for you is most important! When looking for a stylist, you find that it is a very personal thing, like when you are shopping around for a new doctor or dentist.

There are not too many professions around where you need to allow someone to work closely with you and invade your personal space. We all like our space and there needs to be a level of trust established before you are comfortable with people being too close to you or touching your hair.

You know what it is like when you are at a party - you may be having a great time, sipping your drink, watching the party goers and enjoying yourself. That happy, content feeling can suddenly disappear when a stranger comes up to chat to you and chooses to stand so close to you, that you can smell what they had been eating a couple of hours before.

Your personal space can feel invaded and it can feel so uncomfortable that you may even take an involuntary step back and lean back away from that person while talking to them.

In a salon environment you are expected to not only allow a stranger into your personal space, but that stranger also has the power to change how you look and the power to make you very happy or extremely unhappy. That thought alone can be a scary thing for a lot of people.

So what makes a great stylist that would be perfect for you?

Check out the following points for things to look out for when looking for a fabulous new stylist and see which ones are the most important to you.

- Friendly, well presented with nice hair themselves
- Great listening skills – you can tell they are interested in what you have to say
- Is interested in your ideas for your hair and offers you suggestions
- Considers your face shape when designing a style cut for you

- Considers your skin tone and eye color when suggesting colors
- Asks about the colors you often like to wear and your personality when choosing the right color combination for you
- Explains what they are doing for you and to your hair and why
- Checks that you are comfortable and happy during the whole time you are there
- Asks enough questions so that you get the finished result you are after
- Checks that you are happy with the results
- Informs you of the best types of shampoos and conditioners for your hair and why
- Tells you what products were used at the basin in the salon on your hair
- Shows you how to apply the products they have chosen to use in your hair - how much to use and where and how to apply it to achieve the same result at home
- Tell you what can help to control frizz in your hair, add body, increase shine, or whatever it is that your hair needs, or what you have asked of them
- Gives you tips on styling your new haircut so that you can do it at home
- Makes you feel comfortable
- Makes you want to return again and ask for them personally

Even though all of the above is what a great stylist should do, that's not always what happens as we know.

So why is that? Surely hairdressers would always want to do the best they can for their clients?

I would say that would be true for most hairdressers – they really would love to create the best style or color they possibly can for their clients each time. In an ideal world, that would happen, but unfortunately we are not there yet!

One reason why hairdressers don't or are not able to give the best service that they can may have something to do with the type of salon they are employed in. (It is also true that some hairstylists get lazy, bored, are in the industry too long, or are not well suited to the job and industry.)

Different salons charge different amounts for their services and also allow differing lengths of time allowable for each type of service.

If you go into a salon where the prices are cheaper and you don't want to pay much for a haircut, then the hairstylist is not allocated very much time to complete each of her client's services.

For example, if you choose a salon where ladies haircuts are priced at only twenty dollars each, the stylist may only have twenty minutes to firstly consult with you and then create the style cut for you. They have to have you shampooed, cut and out the door in twenty minutes, or they start running behind for the next client that is booked in.

Time constraints placed on stylists due to cheap salon prices will often equal a less than fabulous haircut. The stylist may actually be a great stylist, but without enough time to create the style, they are forced to take short cuts to be faster and that often results in a poorer quality haircut for you.

If you were to choose a salon that includes a finish or blow dry with their style cuts, that may be priced around seventy-five dollars, you will get a very different result.

The stylists there are often given forty-five minutes to an hour to complete your service. This allows plenty of time for a thorough consultation as well as a well-designed haircut and professional finish.

This also allows for you to have the added bonus of being able to watch the stylist dry your hair into a style. You then have the opportunity to ask the stylist for tips on products and how to style your hair easily. The stylist can also check your haircut again once it is dry, and adjust it where necessary to create the perfect individualized look for you and your hair.

So the amount of time allocated for services and overheads of the salon is why there can be quite a difference in the finished results and price between salons.

10. Avoiding Hair Disasters

A hair disaster is one of the scariest things we can imagine.

We all know what a hair disaster is – something that you hate about your hair that is going to take a long time to change into something that you like again.

It could be something as simple as a fringe that was cut too short for your liking, or a strange and unflattering style you are forced to endure on your cousin's wedding day as her bridesmaid.

Maybe your stylist forgot to check the ends of your hair were the same length as the other side and there's an inch or two difference in length between the two sides.

Or perhaps a large chunk was accidentally hacked off your hair at the back where you may not notice it - as this picture shows.

These are only mild hair disasters which we can get over without too much fuss, but I have seen some disastrous haircuts that would need a lot more time in fixing up or growing back after an uneven too short haircut.

Whoever said that the difference between a good haircut and a bad one was only two weeks hasn't had a really bad haircut yet, or they would realize that there are a lot more weeks to wait than only two, until you are happy with your hair again.

Other more serious hair disasters would be a frizzy over-processed perm, terrible color results (perhaps an undesirable patchy green color or blobs of bleach bleeding onto your scalp). One of the worst a 'chemical haircut' which is when your hair is weakened o much by color processes that the hair actually breaks off.

Whatever the hair disaster, it can have a major impact on you. The first hair disaster I saw in the industry stays clear in my mind even over twenty-five years later.

It was when I was new to the hairdressing industry – a first year apprentice with only about six months experience.

It was in the Eighties which was the pinnacle of the perming era. Almost everyone had one and if you didn't then you were just not up with the latest fashion!

It started as a regular day in the salon until Sue came in to have her hair colored. She wanted it as light as possible I learnt, as I listened in to the consultation with the hairdresser. I loved listening in to these conversations, it was a great way to learn new things about hair and I was very excited to be learning to be a hairdresser.

Colleen, the qualified stylist asked Sue all sorts of questions about previous services she had done on her hair, because Sue wanted to change her hair from a mousey brown to bleach blonde.

After completing a thorough consultation and finding from Sue that she had all natural hair with no color or perm in it that she could think off we were ready to color.

Colleen mixed up the bleach and instructed me on how to apply the color. We both applied it, with Colleen checking the whole head all over once we had finished applying the bleach. We put on the timer, checked the hair throughout the processing and all was looking great for Sue's new color.

That was, until I went to rinse Sue's hair at the basin. I warmed the water; made sure she was comfortable and started rinsing.

Suddenly I realized that not only was I rinsing the bleach out of her hair, but that quite a bit of her hair was being rinsed into the basin along with the color!

I was totally horrified!! Here I was, new to hairdressing, following all the instructions to the letter and expecting Sue's hair to be rinsed and shampooed as normal.

Instead I found myself clutching at handfuls of damaged newly bleached hair that was now clogging up the basin drain!

Thoughts raced through my head as I tried not to panic or the client would panic as well.

I calmly massaged a conditioning treatment into the remainder of Sue's hair and told her I was going to leave it in for a few minutes for her.

While she was relaxing at the basin, blissfully unaware, I quickly gathered up the handfuls of hair from the basin drain and with my heart pounding went to show Colleen the disastrous results.

Colleen was also horrified and had the unenviable job of having to tell Sue what had just happened to her hair. As you can imagine there was tears and wailing when Sue realized that the bottom four inches of her hair had just broken off.

I can remember feeling relieved that I was only the apprentice and that it was poor Colleen that had to break the bad news. The reason for the disaster was a simple. It certainly wasn't Colleen's consultation that had failed, or my fault for incorrectly applying the color, or the product being left on too long. Sue had forgotten to tell us that she had had a perm done about eighteen months ago and didn't realize that some of the old perm would still be in her hair – so didn't mention having the perm to Colleen.

Sue actually caused the problem by not telling her stylist of the old perm in her hair at the bottom four inches of her hair. Because part of Sue's hair had perm still in it, that part of her hair was much weaker than the rest of the hair.

The bleach being on that section of hair that had already been weakened by the old perm was too strong for the hair. While processing, the bleach got to the right color on the ends, but broke too many of the hairs bonds that held it together. Sue's hair was weak and broke along the line of between the old perm and natural hair.

This didn't help Sue, who had to endure months of conditioning treatments and a much shorter hair cut than she'd have liked. All because she forgot to tell her hairdresser about a service she had had done over a year earlier.

It's amazing how easy a disaster can happen, so it's a great idea when changing your hair color, or having a perm service to think about exactly what your hair has endured so far.

SECRET STYLING TIP #8

Always tell your hair stylist about any colors, bleach or chemicals you have put in or had done to your hair even if it was months ago, to help you to avoid having a hair disaster.

If you go into a salon with brown hair and forget to tell your stylist that you used to have a full head of bleached foils in your hair, but recently changed it to brown, you could be heading for a hair disaster if you haven't informed your stylist before they do your new color.

There are only a certain amount of bonds in your hair that hold your hair together and gives hair its' strength (the same as strong rope is made up of many small strands woven together holding it together and giving it strength).

Each time you have a chemical service on your hair, bonds are broken. By chemical service I mean color, bleach, perming and traditional straightening.

All of these services will break differing amounts of bonds in your hair. This is because the strength of each product differs, and the different hair types.

However, a revolutionary new type of salon treatment to strengthen hair is now available that almost works miracles! Scientists have developed a new product called Olaplex that can repair the broken bonds in your hair. When used by your stylist in conjunction with the coloring process, Olaplex can actually stop damage occurring in your hair!

If your hair condition suffers badly from damage inflicted by coloring it, ask your stylist if their salon has Olaplex. There is a powerful in-salon treatment performed by hair stylists, as well as an Olaplex #3 treatment to use at home to maintain your hair strength between salon visits.

There have already been copy-cat products produced, but they are not exactly the same as Olaplex, as the secret ingredients of this wonder product are fiercely protected.

To give you more of a guide on the damage caused to hair with chemical services, I have compiled a table with information on what each color does and how much damage it can cause.

You can use the following Coloring Guide as a guide for yourself to enable you to be more informed about colors, and gage possible damage and risks of colors, bleaches and perms on your own hair. If you have bleach on your hair, the most damaging of all, I would definitely recommend you treat your hair to an Olaplex experience!

Hair Color and Damage Guide

Temporary Color	These colors are water based and wash out immediately with the first shampoo. They are great for toning hair a different color for the day or blending gray hair, or hiding regrowth. They are water or mousse based and come in a large range of ready to use colors. **POSSIBLE DAMAGE: NIL**
Semi-Permanent Color	Semis can last from 6 up to 24 washes, and gradually fade out as you wash your hair each time without leaving a strong regrowth line. They blend gray, change tones & darken hair, but don't have the power to lighten your hair. Usually hair is shinier and healthy looking after a semi-permanent color is applied to your hair. **POSSIBLE DAMAGE: NIL to MINIMAL**
Dark Permanent Colors	Color that is darker than your natural hair color. These colors can cover gray hair well, and usually look healthy and shiny. **POSSIBLE DAMAGE: MILD**
Same Level Permanent Colors	These Are great for covering gray, and changing tones in your hair, but still having it look fairly close to your natural color. **POSSIBLE DAMAGE: MILD**

Lighten With Permanent Color	Refers to colors that are 2 – 3 shades lighter than your natural shade and grow out with a regrowth band. **POSSIBLE DAMAGE: MEDIUM**
Lighten With Hi Lift Permanent Colors	Refers to permanent colors that are 4 – 5 shades lighter than your natural shade. **POSSIBLE DAMAGE: MEDIUM – HIGH**
Lighten With Bleach	The lightest color you can get with blonde coloring, resulting from an orange or gold, up to palest lemon and almost to a white color in extreme cases. Often more than one application is needed to lift dark hair to a nice blonde color, which increases the damage done to your hair each time the bleach is applied to your hair. **POSSIBLE DAMAGE: MEDIUM HIGH – EXTREME**
Perms – Alkaline Wave	This is the strongest solution type which is great for strong resistant hair in good condition, but can frizz hair if the solution is left on your hair too long. The solution keeps breaking bonds until it is rinsed from your hair. If it has been on too long, it can then be termed as 'over processed'. This tends to cause your hair to be weaker and frizzy in the result. **POSSIBLE DAMAGE: MEDIUM – EXTREME**
Perms – Acid Wave	This type of lotion is less damaging to your hair than the alkaline solution. It doesn't have the strength to blast your hair open like the alkaline solution does. Often gives a softer more open ended curl, and is less likely to go frizzy. It usually needs heat added to work properly. **POSSIBLE DAMAGE: MILD – MEDIUM**
Traditional Straightening	Most traditional chemical straightening solutions are made quite strong so that they will be effective on very curly hair. If the stylist is careful in their application it can look fantastic, and get either a softening of your curls, or dead straight hair. The solution can be damaging if it is applied incorrectly, or overlapping onto a section of hair that has been previously straightened. They are also very damaging when done on hair that has been colored or bleached previously, as the hair is weaker to start with. **POSSIBLE DAMAGE: MEDIUM – HIGH**

While on the subject of color perm and straightening, there is one other newer type of 'chemical' straightening on the market that is worth a mention

This new straightening method uses Keratin as its base, which is what your hair is actually made from. The Keratin straightening products can slightly improve your hair's condition. I didn't add it into the chart above in the damage area because of it being a different type of product that can add strength to your hair rather than damage it.

There are some rules and restrictions to follow though to keep it looking great and lasting as long as possible (up to three or four). If you follow your stylist's instructions, and use the right sulfate free shampoo that is recommended to be used after this service, then your Keratin based straightening will last for much longer.

As you can see from the guide to hair damage, bleach is by far the most damaging of all colors to the hair, which is why hairstylists tend to be more cautious when applying it as it is a product that keeps working as long as it is left on your head. So you must use bleach with caution and consider the benefits of using Olaplex.

Sometimes I think hairstylists forget the amount of damage that can be done not only to the client's hair, but also to their scalp. Many people can have a strong reaction to the bleach on their scalp, while others experience only a mild tingling sensation on their scalp.

A strong reaction could be redness, itching and skin broken and bleeding, so it is something you want to avoid if possible.

I remember watching a television program where a cosmetic surgery tummy tuck went horribly wrong. The woman was left with a horrendous triangular open wound below her navel, which was oozing pus and watery looking blood and refused to heal.

That was a dreadful disaster which was followed by another about Claire, an attractive girl in her mid-twenties with shoulder length hair, who decided to have blonde highlights done in her hair. The salon stylist decided to use a streaking cap on Claire's head.

For those of you who don't know what a streaking cap is, it's a rubber cap that has rows of small holes all over it that used to be more popular before the use of foils.

The cap fits snugly over your head onto your dry hair. The stylist then uses a small hook to pull small amounts of hair through each hole in the cap and this is the hair that is colored, while the rest of your hair and scalp stays protected and dry underneath the rubber cap.

In Claire's case, they had used the cap and applied bleach to the hair as usual. The stylist wrapped up Claire's head in plastic so that the bleach didn't dry out, and then put Claire under the overhead heat lamps.

As Claire was sitting under the heat lamps, relaxed and reading a magazine, she felt the lamps were feeling too hot on her head. She called the stylist but was assured everything was fine.

As top of Claire's head became hotter she was reluctant to call the stylist only minutes later and suffered in silence until the agonizing pain was too much to bear and again she called the stylist. After checking the color, the stylist immediately took Claire to the basin and rinsed the bleach out of her hair but the painful burning on her scalp continued.

Once she was returned to her seat she could see a red patch on her scalp about the size of a child's palm, but the stylist assured her it would be fine.

When Claire woke next day her scalp was still very sore but when she caught sight of herself in the mirror she screamed in horror.

The red patch on her scalp was even more inflamed, the skin was broken in several places, was weeping and tufts of hair were coming out of the inflamed area.

Claire was horrified and immediately sought medical advice. The heat from the lamps had liquefied the bleach and seeped through a large hole or tear in the rubber cap burning into her scalp.

Chemical burns are just as terrible as other burns and can have long lasting devastating results. In Claire's case the hair never grew back on the affected area.

Once her skin healed, surgeons inserted a small saline filled 'balloon' into Claire's scalp, and then added more saline regularly to stretch the skin as much as possible. (As you know none of us have much extra skin naturally occurring on our scalps normally!)

Once the skin had been stretched enough Claire had her final operation when surgeons cut away the burnt, non-hair producing skin then skillfully stretched Claire's newly created skin together to cover the area of skin removed then stapled the edges together.

It was a long arduous process which had a massive impact on Claire and how she felt about herself. You can imagine that she could have been put off having colors again for the rest of her life!

The salon was sued I believe and her expenses paid but you cannot measure what cost there was to Claire and her confidence and self-esteem. Not to mention the embarrassment of having a large oval shaped bump on top of your head for months.

Thankfully things like that don't happen too often! At least if your hair goes green unexpectedly from a color, your hairdresser can fix it for you. If it is dried out or frizzy from having colors or perms, strength and moisture can be added, avoiding or minimizing a potential hair disaster.

I'm happy to say I have never seen this type of thing happen in any of the salons I have worked in over many years of hairdressing. However, if there is an inexperienced or unqualified stylist or person that wants to do something chemical to your hair, or if you want to do your own hair, beware! Hair colors and bleaches can be dangerous chemicals if you don't know what you are doing with them.

So to ensure you never have a hair disaster, talk to your stylist, discuss ideas and ask them about the possible damage factor of the products on your hair.

It's not worth being a bleached blonde if your hair is going to break off in uneven clumps!

Also home coloring tends to attract more disasters than salon professionals, coloring your own hair can end up costing twice as much in the end if it is a disaster and you have to pay a professional to fix up the unwanted results.

So be smart with your hair to avoid any possible hair disaster and choose professionals who are good at what they do to make sure you will be happy with the end results.

11. So, You Want Big Hair?

It's amazing how time flies, and before you know it fashion is repeated! I was excited when I got my first request for big hair after having many years of everyone only wanting smooth sleek flat hair.

What is "Big Hair"?

The term 'big hair' really just means that you want lots of volume and fullness in your style and height on the top of your head. Usually I find it is girls with medium to long hair that need tips in getting big hair for themselves.

One of my clients, a great father with four teenage girls called me with a problem.

"Remember my youngest daughter, Stephanie?" he enquired.

I did, she was a gorgeous 14 year old with a mass of long dark golden brown hair at the time.

"She decided she wants big hair and the school, as well as her mother and I are not happy with the result." he said. I wondered what on earth she could have been doing.

He went on to tell me about her big hair styling regime.

"She thinks that if she just doesn't comb her hair it will matte up and be permanently big hair!" he explained. "What can you do to help?"

I had to chuckle to myself... my first teenage big hair request after many years... I was certainly up for the challenge!

That afternoon, when she came to see me, I could see why my client was concerned.

The whole crown area of her beautiful long wavy hair was definitely big, but it looked like a matted birds nest and if left much longer would need to be cut out, rather than be combed out.

After much discussion while combing the dreaded dreadlock tangles out of her hair, we explained to her why that was not really the best way to get the big hair that she wanted!

Best Tips for Big Hair:

Get the Right Hair Cut

It is essential to have your hair cut in the right shape to achieve a big hair look, because if you wear your hair all one length, then it is going to be impossible to achieve any height on the top without teasing the roots of your hair first.

What you need to ask your hairdresser for is to put some layers in your hair. When you have shorter layers especially on the top of your hair, your hair is not as heavy on top, and it is the first step to help you get your big hair style.

The other thing you want your hairdresser to do is to add some texture to your hair.

Adding texture to your hair on the top simply means that the hairdresser will intermittently cut or chip small sections of your hair shorter (usually in the mid-lengths and ends of your hair on top of your head) than the actual length of your hair cut.

The reason to get this done is that the shorter pieces of hair help support the longer pieces to stay up for longer and makes it much easier to get your big hair style to work.

Finding the Right Products

The difference between products is massive and you need to choose the right one for your style. Many years ago there was not much choice at all – mousse and hair lacquer were the only things that really worked in getting and keeping a big hair style.

Now, there are hundreds of products available on the market and it is hard to know what to choose. Some of the best products to achieve your big hair look are still mousse and hairspray but now we have more choices available suitable for different hair types.

I recommend volume sprays, curl boosters, styling sprays and root boost products as great 'big hair' products, as well as mousse and hairspray to different clients.

To achieve the best results make sure you get the right product for your hair type.

Best Product Tips for Different Hair Types:

Fine Hair

- Root boost sprays (These often have an extended sprayer which allows you to specifically direct the product onto the root area)
- Volumising products
- Strong hold styling sprays (Use these in moderation)
- Medium hold conditioning mousse (not containing alcohol)
- Shine spray (Spray this only as a mist into the air and then walk under it, do not spray it directly on the hair.)
- Strong hold hairspray or Lacquer

Medium Hair

- Medium hold styling sprays
- Medium hold mousse
- Shine serum
- Strong hold hairspray or Lacquer

Coarse Hair

- Light to medium styling spray
- Shine serum
- Medium to strong hold hair spray
- Leave in moisturizer for the ends (If your hair tends to frizz)

Wavy or Curly Hair

- Medium hold mousse
- Leave in moisturizer
- Medium hold hair spray
- Curl boosters (If you have a bit of a wave these are great products to help you encourage your curls.)

Easy Styling Tools for Big Hair

The styling tools you need to get your big hair style happening are very simple.

If you have even the slightest wave in your hair, all you will need is a great hairdryer (without the nozzle attached) and your fingers to style your hair.

If your hair is straight you will also need a medium to large round brush, depending on the length of your layers. If your layers are shorter, then a medium brush will be best.

If your layers are longer you may need a larger round brush to style with, or a tail comb to tease the roots of your hair with.

TAIL COMB

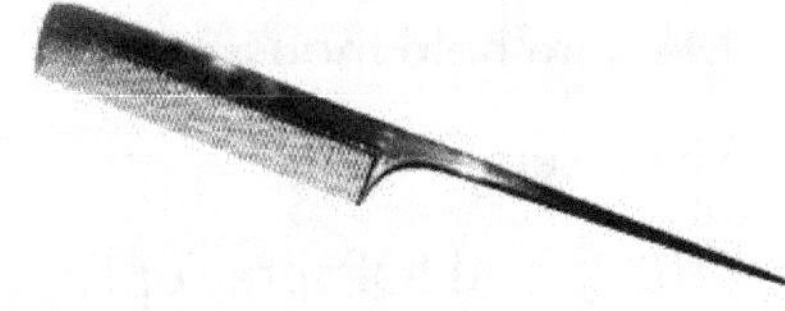

MEDIUM ROUND BRUSH

LARGE ROUND BRUSH

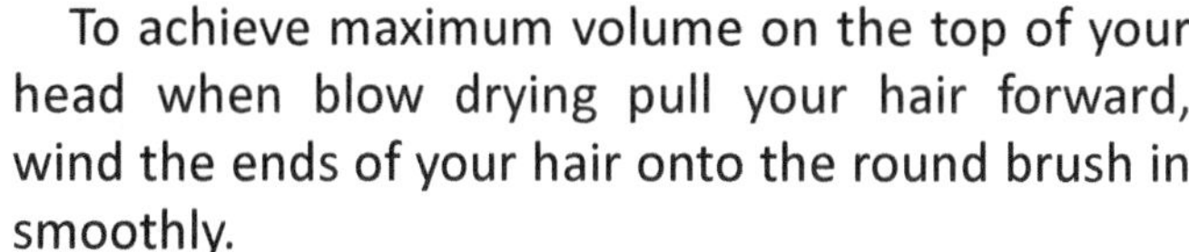

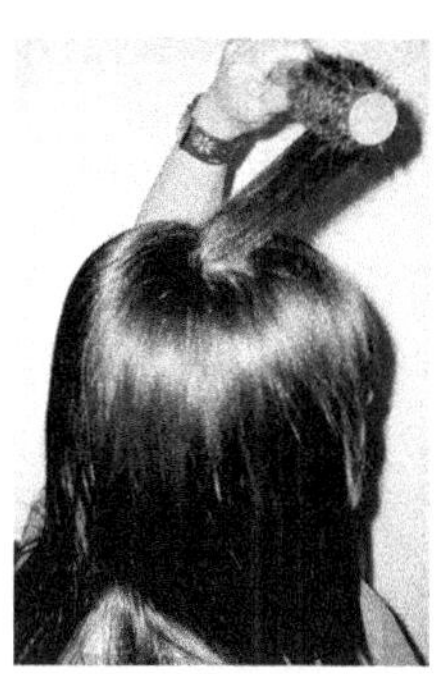

To achieve maximum volume on the top of your head when blow drying pull your hair forward, wind the ends of your hair onto the round brush in smoothly.

Then roll it down towards your head keeping your hair held firmly in the brush.

Keep rolling down until you are a couple of centimeters from your scalp with the round brush above the base of the section of hair you are curling.

Styling Your Big Hair

Once you have the right haircut, products and tools to style your hair, you are ready to style your hair into the big hair look!

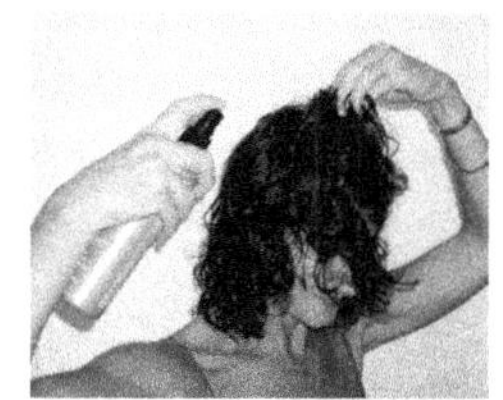

Step 1: Apply the correct products suggested for your hair type (mousse, root boost, styling spray, curl booster etc) to your freshly washed and towel dried hair as per the manufacturer's instructions. (Usually you want the strong hold products applied to the root area of your hair).

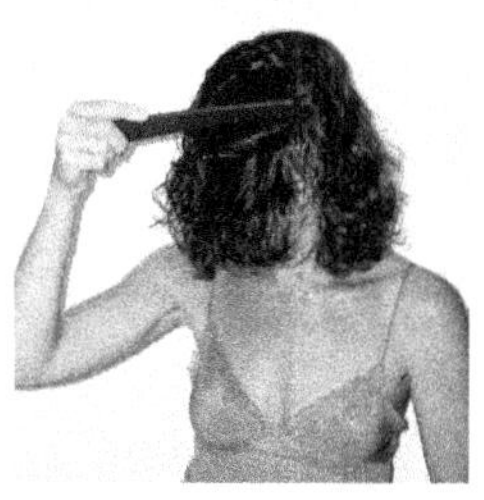

If you have curly or wavy hair, now is also the time to add a leave in moisturizer to the ends of your hair. Comb your hair through with a large toothed comb to distribute the products evenly through your hair... Then shake your head to loosen your hair free.

TIP: *Don't use too much of each product or you may have hair too stiff to move!*

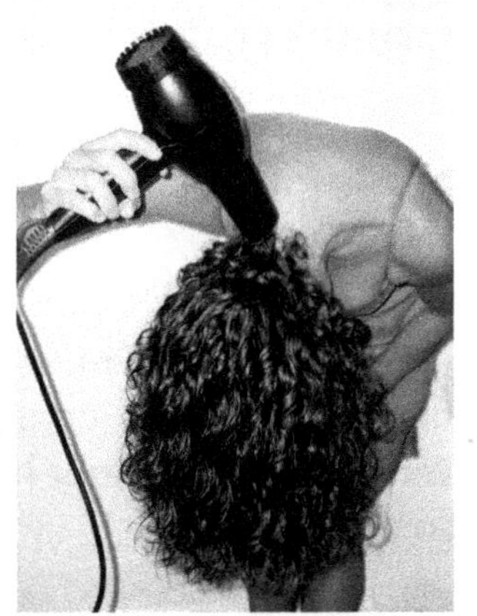

Step 2: Bend over and tip your head upside down so your hair falls towards the ground. Turn on your hairdryer and start drying the root area first.

Use your fingers to help lift the root area of your hair which will encourage the hair to have a lot of body.

TIP: *The reason we concentrate on the root area first to dry, is that it is the area that most of our volume will be coming from.*

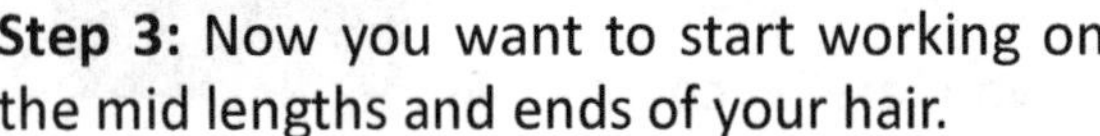

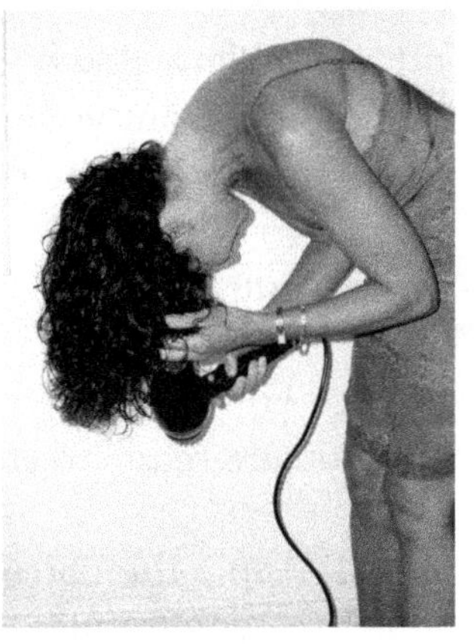

Step 3: Now you want to start working on the mid lengths and ends of your hair.

In the same position with your head upside down, gather your hair by cupping your hand, and scrunching the hair in your hand while drying it with the blow drier.

TIP: *By directing the air flow of your drier into the scrunched hair in your hand, it will help your hair to curl or wave, and give volume to the ends of your hair style with much less frizz.*

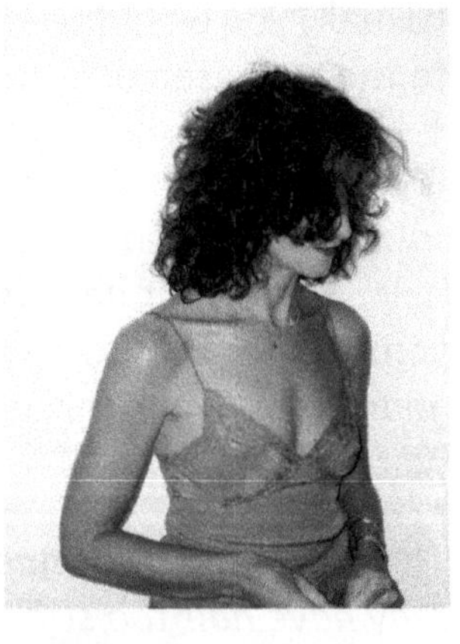

Step 4: Continue working on each section of your wet hair, gathering and scrunching it in your hand until your hair is 90% dry.

Once you reach this stage, turn off your blow drier, and flip your hair back over as you bring your head into the upright position.

When you look in the mirror now, you should see lots of volume in your hair, and the first stage of styling is complete.

Step 5: Next, you want to minimize the frizz if there is any, and have a great shine to your hair. This is simple to do with the right products. I would use a liquid shine spray misted lightly over fine hair, or a shine serum scrunched into the ends of medium or coarse hair.

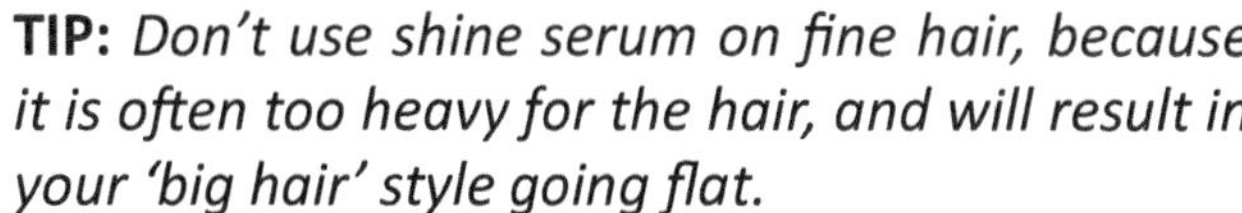

TIP: *Don't use shine serum on fine hair, because it is often too heavy for the hair, and will result in your 'big hair' style going flat.*

Step 6: The finishing touches to your style involve your round brush. If you are lucky enough to already have wavy or curly hair, you may not need to do this step, and should already have a gorgeous mane of big hair!

If you are one of the ones not so lucky, you may have to style the fringe and front area with a round brush to smooth and curve your hair there to match it in with the rest of your style.

Once you have completed this step, and are happy with the look of your big hair style, the last thing you need to do is to give your style a final spray with hairspray or lacquer to hold it in place for the day.

Step 7: The next thing you want to do is to keep your big hair there! Who wants to spend lots of time creating a great big hair look only to have it collapse as soon as you walk out the door?

This is where hair spray and lacquer come in handy. Spray the correct hairspray or lacquer (depending on your hair type and length) to your hair while in the upside down position.

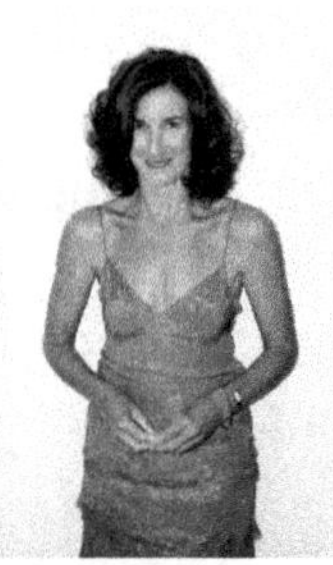

TIP: *Don't use too much lacquer yet or you may look like you have had a fright!*

This will help the spray to get into the layered area and root sections underneath your hair for a longer lasting result, rather than just spraying the top layer of your hair.

Flip your head upright then, and arrange your style around your face to compliment your face shape. (Always try to achieve a shape that makes your face appear oval. This is the most flattering and attractive to the human eye).

These styling steps are highly effective in helping you to achieve the fabulous BIG HAIR that you want!

It really helps when you find a stylist that will go through the steps of styling to create the look you want. Then you are much more likely to be able to duplicate the look yourself at home, which is what we all want.

SECRET STYLING TIP #9

To achieve great volume at the roots of your hair always use a root boost spray before drying your hair, and dry your hair with your head flipped upside down. This will make it easier on your arms, and help you to achieve maximum volume. To finish, blow a cool shot of air at your roots once they are dry while your head is still upside down. Use hairspray or lacquer for a long lasting hold.

12. The Shiny Straight Dream

Have you ever watched those television advertisements that parade gorgeous long haired models with the most glossy, silky straight hair you have ever seen and wonder to yourself: "Why doesn't *my* hair ever look like that, and how does she get it looking so fantastic?"

Often the advertisement is for hair products, showing you a gorgeous models hair, fresh from the full treatment with a professional stylist. The hair is always blow dried and straightened with a myriad of extra products, not shown in the ad (and often not even the brand that is being advertised.).

Your hopes soar while watching the ad, as you think finally; *this* is the wonder product to help me achieve straight, shiny gorgeous hair! Upon the purchase and use of the promised miracle products, you are disappointed, and often don't get anywhere near the result that the ad promised.

Disillusioned, you toss the failed miracle products to the back in the bottom of the bathroom cupboard. (Along with everything else we have bought for our hair and either not used, or used with disastrous results!)

Fear not, seekers of the sleek shiny dream!

This chapter is here to dispel all myths and give you a straight forward, easy way to get your hair sleek, straight and shiny. My aim is to help you to get the best result possible with the least effort!

I will also answer those questions you may have on keeping your hair healthy when straightening and how to get shine immediately and easily if your hair is naturally dull.

The most important thing when straightening your hair to achieve the sleek, straight and shiny dream is to have the right tools and products.

Busting the Myth!

Many girls and women think that choosing the correct shampoo and conditioner will help them get their dream hair but this is not entirely correct.

It is true that there are some fantastic, scientifically developed shampoos and conditioners on the market today in salons. They can help increase the volume or shine of your hair, increase moisture levels to help de-frizz your hair, protect your color from fading, or add protein which strengthens your hair.

Good shampoos and conditioners can even help control the 'fluffy bits' on the top of your head, but none alone will give you the sleek, straight and shiny result you are after.

Getting Started!

The first thing you need to do is to ensure you have the correct styling tools and products.

Essential Tools You Will Need Are:

A Good Quality Straightening Iron

I find the best type of straightening iron is a narrow width ceramic plated iron. There are many good brands available from salons or online.

My reason for choosing a straightening iron with a ceramic plate helps to calm the ions in your hair that cause the frizz and if dropped they won't break like irons with full ceramic plates.

TIP: *Always choose a narrow width iron (1 to 2 inches wide). It is the easiest type of iron to maneuver, and when working close to your scalp you are less likely to burn yourself.*

It is also easier to straighten your hair closer to the root area and great for straightening short hair too!

Thermo Protective Spray

"What is that exactly?" I hear you ask.

A thermo protective spray is simply a product designed to protect your hair from losing too much of its natural moisture content.

It is specifically used with hot electrical tools that can be very damaging to hair when used often. This protective spray minimizes the damage straightening irons can cause your hair.

TIP: *Don't use too much protective spray on each section of hair you straighten – a light mist roots to tips is enough. If you notice steam rising from your hair don't be alarmed – it's simply the thermo protective spray evaporating with the heat.*

HAIR DAMAGE WARNING TIP: If you use your straightening irons without applying a protective spray to your hair, you could be doing your hair some serious damage!

If you notice steam rising from your hair and haven't used a heat protecting product, then it is your hair's natural moisture that is evaporating and being lost.

When moisture loss occurs, frizz and splitting of your hair increases and permanent lasting damage is done.

Tail Comb

A tail comb will make the process of straightening and sectioning your hair much easier. The tail comb looks like a regular comb with a tail for sectioning your hair with.

It is important to ensure your hair is combed thoroughly and free of tangles before you use the straightener on each section.

TIP: *You can use the tail end of the comb to help you section your hair before straightening. The comb end is best used to hold and comb the hair through, and you immediately follow with the straightener.*

Shine Spray

The glossy shine spray is important in the finishing of the straightening process. It gives your hair more shine than just the thermo spray and straighteners, and it can help in calming the fluffy short stray hairs, as well as being a good detangling product.

It is imperative that you use the correct amount in the right area, or you will look like you have oily or wet hair.

TIP: *For best results with your shine spray, mist the spray into the air above head level in front of you, and then walk under the mist.*

If you have extremely fine hair that tends to look greasy quickly or blonde hair, then mist the shine spray onto the ***mid-lengths and ends only*** *from about 20 – 30cms away.*

Hair Clips

Clips will definitely make your straightening experience easier!

By hair clips, I mean large clips that you can use to hold the hair you are not straightening out of the way. Alligator clips are good too - really any clip that is easy to use and can hold up at least half your hair without falling out.

TIP: *Don't try to use hair bands instead! It will slow you down and make the job tedious instead of fun and easy.*

Clips might be small but they are an integral ingredient to easy, fast hair straightening!

Styling Your Hair Straight

Preparation of Your Hair

Hair that is clean, dry and product free to start with is ideal. I always start with completely dry hair for best results. There are two ways you can achieve this.

One is to let your hair dry naturally, the second is to dry your hair on medium to low heat with a blow drier first (preferably with a mist of heat protecting product on your hair first).

For best results if your hair is quite curly, first add some straightening balm to your hair while wet. When drying your hair, use your fingers to pull and smooth your hair out especially at the root area to make it easier for yourself when straightening.

TIP: *To ensure some volume at your roots, pull your hair out at a 90 degree angle from your scalp and dry the root area of your hair first. Straight sleek and shiny doesn't have to mean flat hair with no body!*

Fixing Your Dry Ends

With longer hair, you tend to find the mid-lengths and ends of your hair tend to be drier, fluffy or frizzy, which means there is a lack of moisture in the ends of your hair. This problem is quite common with long hair.

Quite a few of my long haired clients forget how many summers their hair has actually been through. Hair usually grows on average half an inch to an inch (one to two centimeters) per month. If you times that by twelve you will find that your hair grows up to twelve inches (or thirty centimeters) per year.

If the length of your hair is past your shoulders, there's a good chance your long suffering ends have been exposed to a lot of damaging rays and heat since it emerged from the safe haven of your scalp!

Some dryness in long hair that I have seen over the years surprises me. Even enduring only one or two summers can be quite damaging for our fragile hair.

Not only does the sun take out the natural moisture from your hair, being in air conditioning or heating, swimming in chlorine, as well as the hot tools we frequently use on our hair are all contributing factors to our hair being dry and lacking in moisture.

SECRET STYLING TIP #10

Remember that dry/frizzy/fluffy hair = Hair lacking in moisture. This hair needs a leave-in moisturizer daily specific to your type of hair to improve its condition.

Whereas fragile/breaking/split hair = Hair lacking in protein and strength. For best results this hair needs a protein based daily leave in treatment.

Using a leave-in moisturizer on a regular basis can help minimize frizz, slow your hair from splitting, and make it feel and look healthier immediately. It's a fantastic product that is available in many brands and strengths. Fine dry hair may only need a light moisturizer on the ends, whereas curly, coarse frizzy hair would benefit from a heavier leave-in moisturizer with an anti-frizz element, or humidity control benefit.

If you have problems with dry ends, or if your hair likes to go fluffy; then I would add a small amount of leave-in conditioner or moisturizer to the dry areas.

How? Always use a 5 to 10 cent piece worth of your product to start with and spread the product out on your fingers ready for application.

Apply your leave-in moisturizer predominately through the ends of your hair, then lightly through the mid-lengths. If your hair is super dry and fluffy on the top, then lightly brush your hands over the top of your hair once there is almost no product left on your hand. This will ensure you can de-frizz without making the top of your hair look greasy or oily.

1. Section Your Hair Ready to Begin

The first section you want to straighten is the underneath section of your hair, then work your way up to the top of your head, straightening the top layer of your hair last.'

Place the tips of your index (pointer) fingers at either side of your temple next to the hairline about an inch (or two centimeters) above your ears. Draw a line against your head with your fingers around to the center of the back of your head.

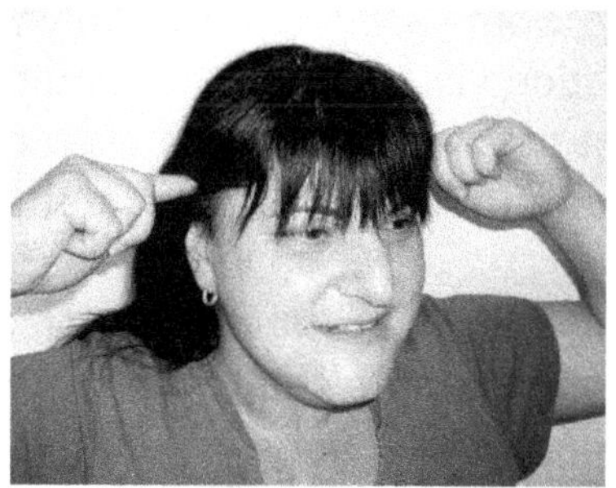

Gather up all your hair above that section made with your fingers, and twist it together before clipping it to the top of your head with an alligator-style clip. You are now ready to start straightening your first section of hair.

TIP: *If you have a lot of hair you may need more than one clip. If your hair is quite short you may also need a few clips to ensure no hair falls down while you straighten the underneath section first.*

2. Apply Thermo Protective Spray

This is one of the most important things you will do – protect the condition of your hair!

When using a thermo protective spray you don't need to use too much. All your hair needs is a light protective coating, not to be drowned in so much protective spray that your hair becomes wet!

Give each section of hair a light mist of the spray just before you straighten that particular section. Repeat the process of light misting on each section of the hair you straighten to ensure that all of it has been protected from the heat of your straighteners.

It's good to know that thermal/heat protective sprays come in different strengths and can do different things.

Some are protective only with no hold at all. Some have a light hold added in and some have quite a strong hold product added to the heat protectant. There are even ones that protect and strengthen, so it is important to find the one that's best for your particular hair needs.

TIP: *Some thermo protective sprays actually make the section of hair go quite stiff straight after the straightening irons are used. This is normal and doesn't mean your hair will feel like it has a lot of product in it, or that it will remain stiff. Simply comb through the straightened hair section once cooled to make it fall natural, and feel silky smooth and soft.*

3. Straightening Your Hair

Now for the fun bit! You have your hair sectioned up ready for straightening and have applied your protective thermo spray; it's time to use those straighteners.

a. Start with one side of your hair above the ear. I recommend that if you are right handed, start above the left ear first. If you are left handed, it can be easier to start on the right side first. Make sure the section you hold up is not wider than the length of the straighteners or some of the hair will fall out for the straighteners.

b. Comb the protected section of hair out smoothly with your tail comb. Lightly mist the section with thermo protective spray, roots to tips. Comb the section again from the roots and stop about half way down the mesh of your hair.

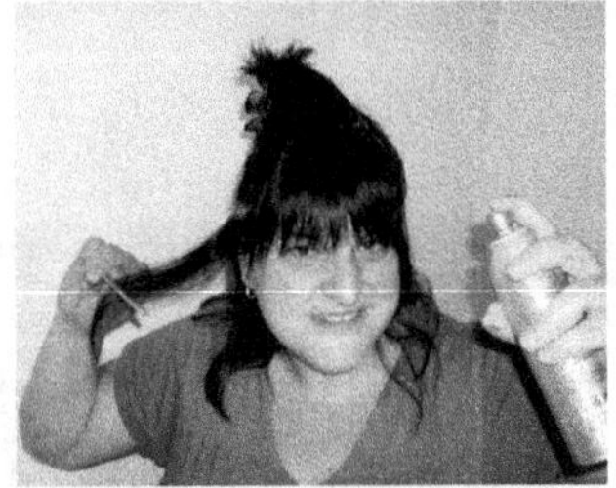

c. With the tail comb still in your hair and your hair held out at a 90 degree angle, insert the section of hair closest to your head (the root area) into the straightening irons and close them around the hair. Holding the straighteners closed around the hair, and horizontal to the ground, slowly run them along the mesh of hair, finishing at the ends.

HOT TIP – WARNING!

Remember to be very careful NOT to touch your scalp with your straighteners when you straighten the root section of your hair near your head.

Straightening irons can pack quite a nasty burn, so be aware and alert when working close to your scalp or ears!

If you do happen to burn yourself (let's face it, we are not always as careful as we should be!) get some really cold water onto the burn IMMEDIATELY and leave on for about 10 minutes, to prevent blistering and provide relief.

d. Still working on the first section (the underneath of your hair), work your way around to the middle of the back of your head. With each section, comb your hair smooth first, apply thermo protective spray, and start straightening at the roots first, through to the tips of your hair with your straighteners.

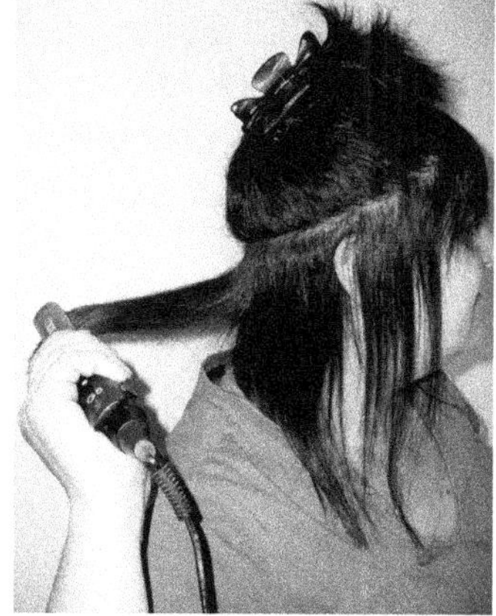

e. Use the comb end of your tail comb each time to hold the section of the hair up and out from your head that you are going to straighten. Using the tail comb at the back of your head in particular makes it easier to hold the section and ensure it is combed free of tangles before the straightening irons are used.

f. Once you have completed one side of your first section and around to the middle at the back, it is time to start straightening on the opposite side. Simply repeat the process of misting, combing and straightening until the whole of your first section of hair is straight.

g. Unclip the clipped up section of your hair. Place your index fingers again at either side of your head at your hairline (near your temple) as before, but this time you want them to be another inch higher than the first time.

Run them around your head against your scalp, (dividing the next section) to meet in the middle of the back of your head. This will give you a section an inch wide right around your head ready to be straightened.

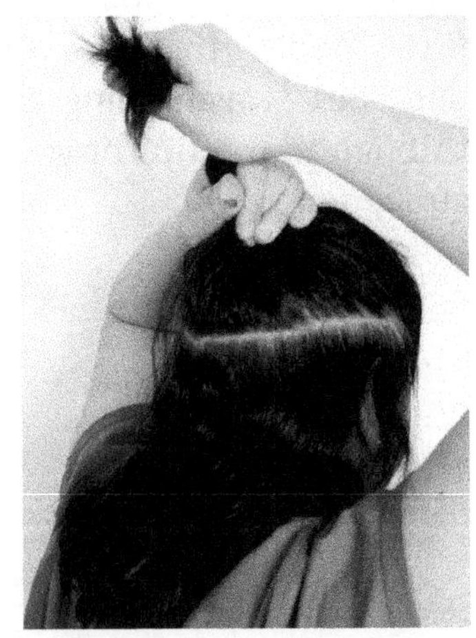

h. Gather all the hair above the section drawn with your fingers, twist it together and re clip it onto the top of your head. You are now ready to start straightening your second section of hair around your head.

i. Continue straightening each section of your hair by repeating the steps below:

Comb your hair section to be straightened smooth and tangle free.

Spray the section lightly with thermo protective spray. Comb again and hold your hair out with the tail comb. Place the root area of your hair into the hot straightening irons. Slowly run both the comb and the straightener down your hair to the ends. Comb through hair once it has cooled down.

j. Repeat this process until you reach the top of your head. With the last section to straighten, ensure it is only half an inch deep at the most.

This will help you get closest to the root area on top and give you a great sleek, straight and shiny finish!

TIP: *Good straighteners these days should only take 10 to 20 seconds to heat up, so turn them on just before you section your hair to start -you don't need to turn them on half an hour before they are needed.*

More Important Stuff You Need to Know About Straightening!

Obviously we all have different hair and hair types, and wants to know more about how to get the best straight, sleek and shiny result possible for our particular hair.

Some girls just have a kink or two to straighten and then they are done, whereas other girls have a mass of curls that are not tamed quite so quickly and easily! (I can see those of you with the curly masses nodding in agreement!)

The curlier your hair is, the shallower the section needed. This will make sure you get it straight right from the roots to the ends of your hair.

So what else is it that you need to know about straightening to sleek, straight and shiny? There is a section devoted to extra questions and answers about straightening in the Questions and Answers chapter, as well as all sorts of other popular questions about hair and products that you may find helpful to know.

13. Flat Iron Curls

The trend is moving from having straight sleek hair every day and evening, to going out with a bit more bounce in your hair.

The right flat irons can be amazing to use to both straighten and curl hair. How do you know if you have the right type of irons or not and what is the right kind?

Generally, the best width of the iron's plates for curling is when they are only one to two inches wide.

The other thing to look at is whether there is a very slight curve to the side edges of the plates, rather than the edges being a sharp right angle. It is the slight curve on the edge of the plates that makes it easier for us to get curls from a 'straightening' iron.

You are able to get different effects depending on what products you use in your hair. If you have only used a thermo protectant spray with no hold, then the curls you create will be a bit softer and tend to drop out or soften sooner.

When you use a thermo protecting spray on hair that has a medium to strong hold in it, your curls will hold for longer and be much bouncier. If you are heading to a formal, wedding or really need the style to hold in, then I would definitely finish with some hairspray or lacquer.

The technique of curling with flat irons is quite simple, but sometimes it can be awkward to perform on yourself, especially as you are looking in a mirror and trying to work with the mirror image of yourself and the irons.

a. Start by dividing your hair straight down the middle of the back, and clip one half out of the way

b. Section using your finger, a horizontal line from the top of your ear to the back center of your head and clip up the top section of your hair. I recommend that if you are right handed, start above the left ear first. If you are left handed, it can be easier to start on the right side first.

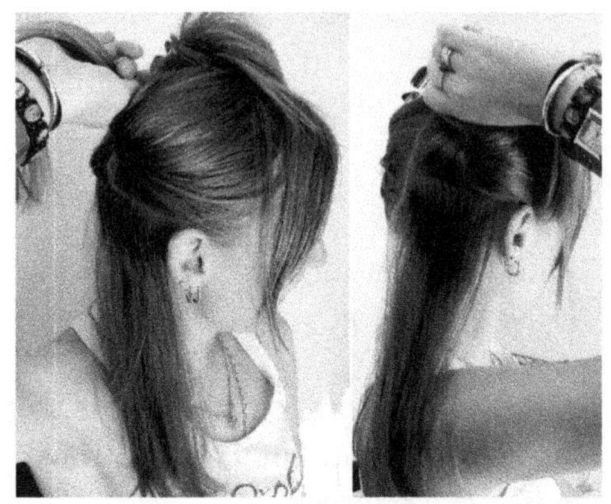

c. Take a vertical section from the center of the back of your head, making sure the section you hold out is no wider than an inch and a half, or your hair will not heat up enough in the center of the section to give you a good even curl effect.

d. Comb the section of hair out smoothly with your tail comb. Lightly mist the section with thermo protective spray, roots to tips. Comb the section again from the roots.

e. With the tail comb still in your hair and your hair held out at a 90 degree angle, insert the section of hair closest to your head (the root area) into the vertically held straightening irons and close them around the hair.

f. Holding the irons closed around the hair, and vertical to the ground, **twist them 180 degrees**, press firmly and slowly run them along the mesh of hair, roots to tips finishing at the ends.

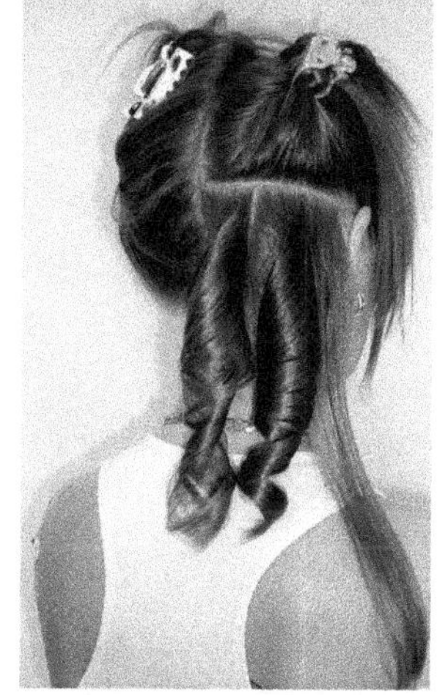

g. Help the hair curl into place after each sectioned is curled, by twirling the hair around your fingers then dropping it. Don't touch your hair until it has completely cooled down.

** You can twist the irons either forward or backwards depending on which direction you would like the curls to go.*

h. Repeat the process of vertical sections, spraying protective product on and twisting the irons so that your hair curls into soft ringlets, working towards the top of the head on the first half of your head

i. Repeat the whole curling process on the other side, starting with the bottom section first.

j. Once your hair has cooled down, you can add some shine spray or drops to your hair on the mid-lengths and end sections, and separate your curls out into smaller strands if you like.

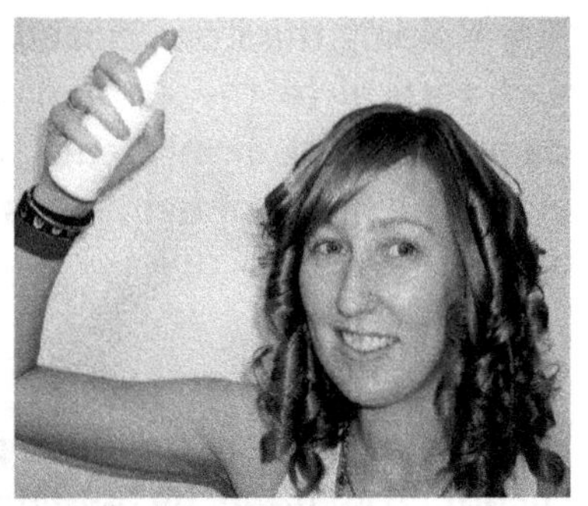

Finished result for curling with your flat irons

Often when curling a full head I like to alternate the way I twisted my irons.

If you would like to finish with your hair curling away from your face, then twist the iron backwards to achieve that. If you would like your hair to curl forward around your face, then twist the irons forward towards your face.

Another tip is that when you reach your top layer, you may find it too much to curl your hair from the roots to the tips.

For a softer effect keep the roots straight and only twist the irons to curl when you're about halfway down the length of your hair to make the curl start further down.

14. Answers to Common Hair Questions

There are a lot of questions about hair that I have been asked, and often many times over.

To help you find answers to questions that you may have about your hair, I have included this chapter which answers all of the most common questions I have been asked over the years.

Hair Condition:

Q: How can I make my hair healthier?

A: There are a few things that you can do regularly to increase the condition and health of your hair.

1. *Give your hair regular conditioning treatments.* I would recommend that through the winter months that you would only need to treat your hair once a month unless your hair is in very poor condition. In spring and autumn, do treatments twice a month and in the most damaging time of summer, treat your hair once a week to maintain great condition. If you find it's more the mid lengths and ends of your hair that are dry, then apply the treatment to that area mainly, rather than at the root area.

2. *Identify whether you need a protein treatment, or a moisture treatment, or both!* Protein gives your hair strength, whereas moisturizing treatments add moisture to your hair.

If your hair is *chemically damaged* from color, bleach or perms, and appears fragile and breaking, then you need a *protein based treatment* to add strength to your hair (yes salon protein treatments are usually stronger and more effective than supermarket ones) I usually don't like to name products because there are so many great ones on the market, but one of the best daily use strengthening products I have ever used is Redken's Extreme Anti Snap.

If your hair is *mechanically damaged* from overuse of hot styling tools, or naturally frizzy or coarse, then you need a *moisture based treatment*. Adding moisture decreases frizz, tames unruly curls, and stops fluffiness. Of course you may need both protein and moisture added to your hair and there are treatments available for that too. The best treatment you can get if you need an extra boost is in the salon. The professionals have the advantage of salon only products, which can be stronger and more effective than anything sold on the shelves.

Ask your stylist about an in salon treatment and what types they have available, and they can correctly diagnose the most effective treatment for your hair. For the best internal strengthening treatment, I'd recommend an in-salon Olaplex treatment.

3. *Don't over use your straightening iron* – that drains moisture from your hair quickly, always protect your hair before straightening with a heat protectant product. Ask your stylist which temperature setting is best for your hair type.

4. *Use your blow dryer on a medium setting, not on high to style*. Lots of women have powerful hairdressing quality driers these days. If you use the highest heat setting, and don't constantly move the dryer around, you will fry a piece of your hair very quickly, and there's nothing that can fix that piece of hair then… apart from growing it out or cutting it off!

Q: I get a lot of breakage, and have been getting my hair bleached for a while now. Why does my hair break in certain areas and how can I stop it?

A: It is very common for bleached hair to break easily. Bleaching is the most damaging type of coloring that we can do to our hair. It breaks bonds that hold your hair together internally. When too many bonds are broken in one point of your hair, it causes a weak spot that is prone to breaking. It can then easily be broken by something as simple as brushing your hair.

Weak spots are mainly caused by bleach applications overlapping each other, or pieces of hair being bleached more than once in the same spot, or even through the use of a hot styling tool on a damaged area for too long can cause the hair to have more bonds broken and weaken more.

The most common place for breakage is around the sides and hairline of the face, and the crown area. The crown area can be a 'hot spot' or may have had the bleach on for the longest. The first inch or two of hair around the sides and front of your hair is finer than on the rest of your head. This means it will process faster than the rest of your hair during chemical treatments like lightening or perming. Because the hair there is finer, it can be damaged more easily than the rest of your hair.

To stop it breaking and improve condition:

1. Use the best protein treatments you can find as well as a daily strengthener.
2. Use hot styling tools as little as possible.
3. Ask your hairdresser to be careful when applying bleach on your hair and let them know it tends to break.
4. Change your color, wait longer between applications or stop over-bleaching your hair.
5. Get regular professional Olaplex treatments done in the salon, and follow them up with home treatments of Olaplex #3.

Q: I've got curly hair and find my hair looks frizzy all the time, some days more than others. How can I stop it and why is it frizzy?

A: Frizziness is caused through a lack of moisture in the hair. The best way to add moisture is through regular moisturizing treatments and adding a daily leave-in moisturizer into your hair (usually only on the mid-lengths and the ends of your hair).

There are some specific types of moisturizers that are designed specifically or naturally curly hair. They often have the added bonus of humidity fighter ingredients, which help control frizz on a damp or humid day.

Ask your stylist to recommend the right leave-in moisturizer for your hair type to ensure the best results. You can even ask them to demonstrate how and where to use it in your hair.

Q: I'm trying to grow my hair longer, but keep finding split ends. How can I stop the ends of my hair from splitting?

A: Once your hair starts splitting, it will keep splitting further up the hair shaft then break off. The best thing to do is have regular haircuts and cut off the split ends. Also, there are various seal the ends and 'prevent split ends' products.

Find a good one, and apply a small amount to the ends of your hair, which will help it stay healthier. You are still likely to get split ends, (especially with fine hair) but perhaps not as many. When you notice one, you can carefully snip it off with some sharp nail scissors in between haircuts. However my best advice is to make sure you have your ends trimmed regularly to maintain good condition and minimize split ends.

Q: How can I protect my hair and prevent it from being damaged by blow drying and straightening every day?

A: Blow drying and straightening hair, especially every day will dry your hair out and cause damage for sure. The best way to minimize the damage is to protect it with a heat protectant product, regular treatments and regular visits to your stylist for a trim. Try not to use hot styling tools to style your hair everyday – try putting your hair up or pinning it back on the second day.

Q: I work outside a lot with my job. How can I protect my hair from the harsh sun in summer time especially?

A: There are special solar care products available from salons, specifically designed as a sunscreen for your hair. They protect your hair from drying out the same as the sunscreen for your skin protects you from burning.

If you have colored hair, they can help protect your color and minimize fading in the harsh sun. Ask your stylist for a product recommendation.

Solar care moisturizers are usually a light cream that can be applied over wet or dry hair. Of course if you are going swimming, you will need to reapply after swimming, the same as you would with the sunscreen for skin.

Questions about Hair and Scalp Problems:

Q: My scalp is often oily and my ends are dry and dull. What can I do to fix my hair problems?

A: There are two parts to this answer. For an oily scalp, you can choose to use an oily scalp shampoo, and try to only wash your hair every second day. The more scrubbing you do on your scalp, the more blood with yummy nutrients are drawn to your scalp.

This is great for increasing growth of your hair, but not so good for you if you want less oil on your scalp. Increased stimulation of the scalp means your sebaceous glands that produce oil will up the production – something you definitely don't want!

Try using a 'dry shampoo' at your root area. This absorbs oil and helps your hair look fresher and may be an easy way to shampoo your hair less.

As for your dry dull ends, I would recommend you use a daily leave in moisturizer after washing your hair, and apply a small amount on the ends of your hair only. This will add moisture and counteract the dryness. To fix the dullness, use a liquid shine drops product. Only a tiny bit added to your dull ends will add shine instantly where you need it, without adding grease or an oily look to the rest of your hair.

A spray shine product is also a great option but spray this directly on the ends only – not on the top of your hair.

Q: We have a chlorinated swimming pool and my family loves to spend time in the pool. What shampoo should I use in my hair and my children's hair to get rid of the chlorine build up in our hair from swimming?

A: The best thing to help erase the effects of chlorine in the hair, or any minerals that you'd rather not have in your hair is to use a clarifying shampoo. A clarifying shampoo helps dissolve and draws away the chemicals and minerals on the hair.

Lather up the shampoo into your wet hair and leave it lathered in your hair for 5 to 10 minutes. This gives it time to break down stubborn greenness in the ends of blonde hair especially!

If you are able to shampoo the chlorine out of the hair immediately after swimming rather than waiting for hours, you can get a better result in removing the chlorine. Wearing swimming caps can also help minimize damage to hair.

Q: My scalp is dry and itchy, but not all the time. What can I do to stop it from itching and flaking?

A: Often if you experience flaking and itching only sometimes, it can be related to being overly stressed or anxious. Other times it can be a reaction to a new product you have started using, or a reaction to having hairspray sprayed on the scalp, or leaving too much product on your scalp.

There are scalp soothing shampoos on the market that can help with scalp dryness and itchiness when you need them and once your scalp clears up you can just pop them in the cupboard and return to your regular shampoo.

If it is a certain product you are using, or if you're applying too much product onto your scalp, then try changing your methods or products.

If your scalp is only dry and itchy sometimes, I wouldn't choose a dandruff shampoo to use first, as it may be too strong for what is needed – try to find a scalp soothing one which is milder and try it out first.

Q: My hair seems to be falling out more than usual, and I'm worried about it. What can I do to stop my hair falling out, and why is it happening?

A: It is a very worrying thing indeed when your hair suddenly decides to shed more than usual. Every time you brush it, you wonder how much will come out this time, and whether you have some sort of horrible hair loss disease you have never heard of! You worry that it's going to keep falling out until there's none left.

Many clients over the years have asked me about hair loss and why it happened, and will it stop or not.

It is a very common thing to happen, so if it's happening to your hair now, this explanation will be very helpful.

To give you an answer, I first need to explain the three stages of hair growth.

The Hair Growth Cycle

Stage 1. *Growing stage*, where the hair grows on your head for between four and seven years.

Stage 2. *Resting stage,* where the hair goes through a resting period of three to four months, where it doesn't grow but is still alive and attached to your head.

Stage 3. *Replacement stage*, where the resting hair falls out, and a new hair replaces it and begins growth.

This is the regular growth pattern that is repeated over and over again all the time on your head.

The usual amount of hair loss per day is around 75 hairs per day, and that's a normal thing to have happen. It's when we find around 150 hairs per day falling out that we start to panic and wonder what's happening to our hair.

To find the reason for your excessive hair loss, you need to look backwards- about three or four months ago.

Ask yourself what was happening in your life then. Were you under more stress or more anxious than usual? Did you have a baby or an operation and anesthetic? Perhaps you had a shock, or a car accident? Maybe you were having a difficult time at work? Or did a relative or friend pass away?

What you are looking for is a disruption in your life that happened about three or four months ago, that was large enough to cause some of your hair to go into its' resting stage prematurely (Stage 2).

If you find that something happened in your life then that was significant, then that is the likely cause of the excessive hair loss you are experiencing... Don't worry!

If that is what has occurred, then your hair will follow the stages through, and Stage 3, the replacement stage will start, and in a few more months you will have lots of new growth clearly visible in your hair.

If you can't find a reason for your hair loss, and it continues, go and see your doctor for further testing. If you really have a hair loss problem you want checked out, then it is a **Trichologist** that you need to see. A Trichologist is someone who is a specialist in the study and diagnosis of hair problems.

Questions about Colors:

Q: I like my natural color and would like to have a few highlights added. I don't want to have to come in every 6 weeks and I don't want the regrowth to look obvious when the color grows out. What would I ask my stylist for?

A: You would ask your stylist to either do very fine highlights that are only a few shades lighter than your natural color.

Your other alternative if you prefer something a bit bolder and chunky, and have a flat hairstyle with a part in it, is to ask for some splices of blonde underneath your part. The stylist will leave out a centimeter or so of hair either side of your part, and color a splice of hair underneath.

Then when the natural hair is let down, it's like a veil of natural hair with blonde pieces peeking through, rather than ending up with stripes on the top of your head. Low maintenance and looks great – also great for other colors, even something wild and bright!

Q: I have blonde foils and color in my hair. I love it when I come out of the hairdresser and for the first few weeks. After that it seems to go a yellow or gold color though, which I don't like. How can I keep my hair looking great in between my visits to the stylist?

A: The best thing to keep your hair looking great and staying the cool blonde color you prefer is to use a toning conditioner or shampoo.

If it is gold and yellow that you want to stop in your hair, then the toning shampoo or conditioner you will need is a purple color. Obviously you don't want to end up with purple hair, but purple is the opposite of yellow and will counteract the yellow tones in your hair very well. My absolute favorite toning conditioner is Fabuloso Platinum Blonde conditioner by Evo.

Usually you would only need either a purple shampoo or a purple conditioner – you don't need to use both. If you do, the toning could be too strong and you will end up with either purple or gray sections in your hair.

For best results use the toning product once you feel your hair tone has faded to the gold color, not as soon as you leave the hairdressers.

Q: How can I use a toner properly so that I don't end up with purple or gray hair?

A: The undesirable purple or gray tones in blonde hair occur when the toning shampoo or conditioner is too strong. That's why I would recommend only using either the shampoo or conditioner, not both at the same time.

Sometimes though, even using just one of them causes too much purple or gray. What you need to do then, is choose the conditioner to use as a toner and mix it with some regular conditioner. This will water down the strength of the toning, and give you a better result. You may have to experiment with how much of the regular conditioner to add to end up with perfectly toned blonde hair.

Q: I have gray hair at the sides and front of my hair and have it colored regularly. I don't like seeing the grays showing through on the sides and at my part in between having a color. Is there anything I could do to make it look better until I go to my stylist next?

A: Yes, there are a few things you can do. There are colored mousses and other types of temporary color products available that can be used.

If you dot a small amount of colored mousse on the gray regrowth at your temple area and along the part and dry it into your style, it will help blend your color and not be as obvious that your hair color has started to grow out.

Another type of temporary color that's popular is in powdered form – like an eyeshadow. Called Color Wow, it is easy to use and very effective.

The other alternative is to ask your stylist if they can color a 'T' section only for you. What I mean by 'T' section being colored, is to color one to two inches around your front hairline and an inch or so either side of your part.

This works really well as an alternative and is usually cheaper than having your full color done. A lot of clients will have their regrowth colored every six weeks, but at the third week mark come in to the salon for a 'T' section color in-between.

Questions on Products:

Q: How do you use hairspray and lacquer effectively, and what is the difference between them?

A: Firstly, the difference between a hairspray and a lacquer is their strength. Both products are the same in that they are designed as a finishing spray that is usually used at the completion of your styling to hold your style in place.

A hairspray is not as strong as a lacquer. Lacquers were most popular in the eighties, when the styles all defied gravity and you really needed the massive strength of a lacquer to keep your hair creation from flopping.

At the moment, styles are a bit more 'free flowing' and have movement, and would suit using a hairspray only for a light to medium hold.

This is great for every day styling. However, when you have a special occasion and don't want a single hair to move from its designated place, then you can't beat a great lacquer for all day hold. I would always use a lacquer if I was styling for special events like formals or weddings in particular.

Q: Do any of the thousands of products available actually do what they say they will do?

A: Thankfully yes! There are quite a few products that are fabulous, and definitely do what they say they will – it's a matter of finding them.

I always think that the products that work the best and actually do what they say they will are the 'salon only' brands. Yes they are much more expensive than the supermarket or chemist brands, but if it is effectiveness you want, then a recommendation from your stylist is much more likely to do what it says it will, than trying to pick anything off the supermarket shelves and hoping it will work.

Q: How do I use mousse?

A: To use mousse effectively, firstly spray an egg sized amount onto one of your palms. Then spread the mousse between your hands, ready to apply to your hair.

If you have longer hair, it can be easier to apply the mousse with your head upside down and scrunch it into your hair evenly. If you apply it when your head is upright, you tend to get most of the mousse on the top layer of your hair, which is not as effective.

Mousse will give strength and hold to your style and can be great to help hold in a blow dry. Sometimes mousse contains alcohol though, which can have a drying effect on your hair.

Q: Why is my hair dull and not shiny? How can I increase shine in my hair?

A: If you want to increase shine fast in your hair, it can be done in an instant! There are great shine sprays available, as well as shine drops that can give your hair shine immediately.

The reason that some people's hair is shiny naturally, and some are dull naturally isn't always condition of their hair. The outside layer of each hair is called the cuticle layer and it is like little scales on the outside of your hair.

If the scales are lying flat naturally, then light hits the scales, and because it is a flat surface, the light is reflected off the flat surface. This gives the appearance of shiny hair.

If your cuticle layer is not lying flat, then when the light hits your hair, rather than be reflected to appear shiny, the light is absorbed into the hair, so we get the impression of dull looking hair.

Treatments will help smooth the cuticle layer to give you better condition and shine, which is great in the long term, but if it is instant results you want, then a shine spray or serum will work fantastically to add shine immediately.

Q: What product do I use to get my wavy, naturally frizzy hair to be non-frizzy?

A: There are a lot of frizz easing products on the market at the moment, so it's a matter of finding the right one for your hair.

I would recommend using a daily leave in moisturizer from the range available, to add to your hair on a daily basis. However some professional shampoos and conditioners with regular use can actually tame the frizz and smooth down the hair.

I love using Redkens' Smooth Down shampoo and conditioner before you even add any other anti-frizz products. It is moisture your hair needs to fight frizz, so choose a product with little or no styling hold, with anti-humidity properties and moisture to get the best results possible for your hair.

Q: My hair is very fine and limp. What can I do to add more volume and body into it, and have my style last longer?

A: It is definitely worth using a volumising shampoo and conditioner that is designed for fine limp hair to start with. These products are usually lighter, especially the conditioner so they don't tend to weigh your hair down or leave it greasy looking.

The next thing to use is a root lift spray. These are designed for fine hair, and are sprayed at the roots of your hair when it is wet then blow dried in. Body and volume is easily achieved with the strength of these types of sprays supporting your style. If you start your styling by drying the root section of your hair upside down first, then that can help in increasing volume too. I recommend Root Canal by Evo – a great root lift spray that's easy to use.

I'd also suggest using a hairspray or lacquer to finish off your style. This will help set your style in place for the day, and give better hold. I know stiffness is not usually what we want in our hair though! For a more natural feel, once your hairspray has dried on your style; ruffle it about a bit with your fingers, then apply a very light spray over the top of your style to finish. I like to use Silhouette super hold hairspray for this because its strong, fast drying and you don't need to use much.

Q: My hair goes greasy at the roots quickly, but the rest of my hair still looks ok. How can I stop my hair from looking greasy, and how can I go longer without washing my hair and having to restyle it?

A: There are a lot of people that have that problem. Greasy hair always makes you feel less than happy with your hair. There is an easy solution though – dry shampoo!

Dry shampoos are great to use between washes on your dry greasy hair. They absorb the excess oil in your hair, and can be brushed out – no water necessary!

During the sixties, dry shampoos were quite common but not as effective. Most women at that time would only wash their hair once a week, or even only once a fortnight! They would have a weekly or fortnightly hairdressing appointment at a salon, where their hair would be set and styled for the week.

This seems a strange notion now, with so many of us washing our hair every day, or every other day.

Once the free loving free flowing hair of the seventies arrived, then the hair sprayed perms of the eighties, we all needed to wash our hair more often.

Now that there are more styles that can last longer than a day around, dry shampoos are making a comeback, and more companies are cashing in on the trend by releasing their own dry shampoos with finer particles so you can't see it in the hair. For best results I recommend using a salon brand of dry shampoo like either Water Killer by Evo or Moroccanoil dry shampoo, which is available in both light and dark tone.

Questions on Straightening Hair:

Q: Sometimes I straighten my hair in the morning, but it gets damp during the day. Can I do a 'quick fix', and do I need to put more thermo spray on my hair before fixing my kinks up?"

A: If your hair gets damp and goes kinky during the day, there is a quick fix yes!

Your thermo protecting spray is still in your hair from the morning, so if there are only a few wavy bits, I'd isolate them and run the straightener over just the wavy pieces.

If your hair got seriously damp and is looking frizzy, then I would re-mist with the thermo protective spray over the top layer before fixing. This will ensure the hair doesn't lose any of its natural moisture, and help you tame the frizzy areas more easily.

Q: My hair is coarse and quite frizzy and curly. If I follow your instructions will I be able to get my hair really straight and shiny too?

A: If you follow the instructions in the straightening chapter, then yes you will certainly achieve straight shiny hair. The thing I do recommend to girls with really curly frizzy hair is to straighten their hair using more sections that are thinner – half an inch deep rather than an inch deep as in the instructions. This will ensure you get the straighteners close to all the root areas (because this type of hair tends to be quite curly at the root area too).

Also if you hold your hair firmly once it is smooth and tangle free, and have applied your heat protecting spray with a styling hold factor inbuilt, it helps to get a better result too. Be careful not to burn yourself on the scalp when trying to get the kinks at the roots out!

Q: I have seen wet and dry straighteners available in the shops recently, and wondered what they were like?

A: I personally don't like the wet and dry straighteners but not because they don't do a great job of straightening!

When you straighten your hair from completely wet, it is harder to tell if the steam rising from your hair is just water evaporating, or whether the hair is already dry and you are starting to lose some of your natural moisture instead.

I have noticed that clients who regularly use this type of straightening iron over the long term tend to have hair that is suffering more heat damage than others. Often their hair is split up a lot further than just at the ends. Because of the damage, often more length is needed to be taken off than what the client may have desired.

If you leave split ends in your hair they won't disappear. Instead your hair keeps splitting further up the mesh and eventually breaks off. This is something that we definitely want to avoid!

Questions about Styling:

Q: How do I curl my hair easily?

A: There are a few different ways of curling hair – Blow drying with a round brush, hot rollers, curling tongs or straight irons would be the most popular.

You need to choose the tool that is the easiest for you to manage, which suits your length of hair. I'd suggest you borrow a friend's tongs or irons to try first, or get your stylist (or your friend if they are great at using them) to show you how to use the styling tool and figure out which is the easiest for you to maneuver.

Your stylist can advise you on which method will achieve the types of curl you want in your hair too, so don't be afraid to ask them- great stylists are usually very happy to share information with you!

Q: When I straighten my hair, the next day it looks kinky and doesn't seem to last more than one day. How can I get my straightening to last longer than one day?

A: There are a few things you can do to increase the likelihood of your hair staying straight and looking fabulous for more than a day.

1. Use a heat protecting spray that has a strong styling hold built into it.
2. Take shallow sections that are only half an inch deep to work with.
3. Mist the heat protecting spray with hold onto each section before you straighten it.
4. To get right to the roots, hold the hair section out at 90 degrees from your scalp – it's much easier to straighten right at the roots then.
5. Wait until your hair has cooled down before brushing it.
6. Stay away from humidity, rain and any type of water!
7. Fix any minor kink on the second day that you caused through sleeping, and you are looking great for a second day.

Q: When I blow dry my hair, my fringe always goes too curly. Why does it do that?

A: If you are blow drying your fringe with a round brush, and it is going too curly, then the size of your round brush is too small.

Invest in a larger barrel size brush, and you can then easily smooth your fringe out and not end up with too much curl there. It is better not to wind the hair up too close to the scalp too, unless you want lots of volume at the root area of your fringe.

'Up' Styling Questions:

Q: My hair is a medium length. How can I put it up quickly and easily for work other than in a ponytail?

A: A great idea is to use some of the many clips and combs that are available now. For example, a great easy style for medium hair is with an alligator-style clip.

a. First gather your hair together smoothly
b. Twist it into a ponytail at the centre of the back of your head
c. Then twist it tightly so that the ends of your hair are at the top
d. Secure it firmly with an alligator clip
e. Let the ends of your hair fall softly over the clip.
f. Use a bit of hairspray to spike the ends a bit, and make them fan over the clip at the back of your head evenly for an interesting finish.

If your hair is too long for this, try a side plait wound around itself into a bun then secure with bobby pins for a quick easy side bun.

Q: How can I get that professional smooth finish when I put my hair up in a ponytail? I have a lot of shorter bits at the sides that curl and stick out when I put it up.

A: Once you have your pony tail brushed as smoothly as you can, then give your head a spray with hairspray and re brush it into the pony tail.

Secure your hair with a tie, and then spray hairspray on any errant pieces of hair that are not lying smoothly against your head and smooth them back using the palm of your hand. This will help to give you a smooth professional finish every time.

If you have extremely stubborn bits that won't sit flat and smooth, then use lacquer (strong hairspray) on the unruly pieces and smooth the hairs down with your palm.

If there are still a few stubborn hairs sticking out, use your hairdryer and dry the hairspray into the hair in the smooth position. This will help with the most stubborn of hairs!

Q: How can I keep my styling time to a minimum?

A: The best way to keep styling time to a minimum is to firstly towel dry it really well. Then use the hair dryer to take enough moisture out of your hair before you start styling with a brush.

The wetter your hair, the longer it will take to style. Wait until your hair is about 70% to 80% dry before styling it with your round brush and you will notice it is much quicker to style.

Make sure that you always completely dry your style, because if you don't, then your hair will bounce back to its' normal shape before you even make it to lunch! Also remember to protect your hair with a thermo heat protecting spray every time you use a hot drier.

Q: My hair is long and very thick which makes it hard to style. What would be a quick 'up' style that's good for long thick hair?

A: When you have long thick hair, it limits you with up styles, because there is often too much hair to make them work. Styles where there are twists and plaits can be good, because they minimize the amount of hair you have into manageable amounts.

A great 'up style' for long thick hair is a twisted side ponytail. To make it look a bit special, separate a section out from your pony tail, then twist it tightly and wind it around the band of the ponytail and secure it on the underneath side with a couple of bobby pins.

15. Ten Top Styling Tips

SECRET STYLING TIP #1

'When styling your hair, or choosing a new hairstyle, always make sure that the finished style makes your face appear oval shaped.'

SECRET STYLING TIP #2

Always make sure the colors you choose for your hair will compliment, not clash with your natural skin tone, and colors of clothes you favour wearing.

SECRET STYLING TIP #3

To achieve the best results possible always ask your hairdresser to recommend the best shampoo, conditioner or styling product for your particular hair needs. Some great salons will give you a small sample to try for free, so you can see how it works in your hair before you buy the product. Some brand ranges are also available to purchase in a mini size too which is helpful in testing the product on your hair.

SECRET STYLING TIP #4

When using a hot styling tool on your hair always allow your hair to cool down completely before styling, brushing or running your fingers through your dry hair, to ensure a longer lasting hair style.

SECRET STYLING TIP #5

When styling your hair with any hot styling tool protect your hair from moisture loss by using a protective heat shield spray on your hair first. This will help ensure your hair doesn't lose too much of its natural moisture and prevent mechanical damage to your hair.

SECRET STYLING TIP #6

When searching for a new hairdresser, either approach someone that you think has a fantastic style cut or color and ask them where they got it done and who was their stylist, or search online for local salons and stylists who are recommended with pictures.

SECRET STYLING TIP #7

When you bring in pictures of a cut or color you love and want, you have a much better chance of the hairstylist understanding what you like rather than just trying to explain it to them in words alone.

SECRET STYLING TIP #8

Always tell your hair stylist about any colors, bleach or chemicals you have put in or had done to your hair even if it was months ago, to help you to avoid having a hair disaster.

SECRET STYLING TIP #9

To achieve great volume at the roots of your hair always use a root boost spray before drying your hair, and dry your hair with your head flipped upside down. This will make it easier on your arms, and help you to achieve maximum volume. To finish, blow a cool shot of air at your roots once they are dry while your head is still upside down. Use hairspray or lacquer for a long lasting hold.

SECRET STYLING TIP #10

Remember that dry/frizzy/fluffy hair = Hair lacking in moisture. This hair needs a leave-in moisturizer daily specific to your type of hair to improve its condition.

Whereas fragile/breaking/split hair = Hair lacking in protein and strength. For best results this hair needs a protein based daily leave in treatment.

I hope you found this book informative and interesting, and have a new found confidence and ability with styling your own hair more successfully at home now. Happy styling!

www.ingramcontent.com/pod-product-compliance
Lightning Source LLC
Chambersburg PA
CBHW070625310726
48982CB00001B/173

* 9 7 8 0 6 4 8 1 1 1 1 2 2 *